LOVE AND OTHER STRANGE THINGS

BY JENN BRIDGES

Chapter 1

Devon Willis strode down her street with an air of confidence that belied her current anxiety. She wore a gray canvas messenger bag slung over her shoulder and went over the checklist of its contents once again. Inside she carried a full change of clothes, a five-dollar bill, headache pills, a box of matches, and tube socks. Both the box of matches and the tube socks had proven very useful over the course of the past year. More useful than she ever would have imagined prior to her year of darkness. Life was not easy when one was a cursed woman.

Still Devon had reason to be optimistic on this particular day. She had a date, and not one from an app. A real date, with a person she really knew from work. She and Mel from work had been casually flirting for months. Devon worked as a professor in the Psychology Department, while Mel worked with the university's housing office. On Friday Mel had asked Devon out to dinner. There was a new Thai restaurant, which in a place like Nightshade, Massachusetts was a big deal. Nightshade was one town over from Salem. It had an equal amount of dark history, but with none of the tourist attractions.

Devon stood outside Bon Appetit Thai and took a deep breath. Inside had a sleek modern appearance. Low lit purple lighting set the obvious mood. Devon noticed Mel sitting at a booth across the room. The woman stood and waved, a gesture which Devon quickly returned. Mel was beautiful. She wore a vintage looking dress, white with red polka dots. Her hair was done in an updo and she wore glasses that Devon had never seen her in. Mel was quirky but in a cute way.

"Hello, I'm so glad you could make it," Mel greeted, wearing a warm smile.

"Are you kidding I wouldn't miss it. So glad you invited me out."

"I'm glad you're so eager. I don't always get that response." Mel said. Devon cocked her head, hoping she wasn't being obvious.

"I'm sorry to hear that. I can't imagine anyone giving you a bad response," Devon said.

"You'd be surprised. Some people just don't value an opportunity when it's presented to them." Something about Mel's wording struck Devon funny. Maybe Mel was feeling nervous. The server came and Devon put in her order for drunken noodles. When the server left she glanced up only to find Mel staring at her with an intense look over her face.

"Are you ready to get this started?"

"I thought we already were getting started."

"Well, you haven't even heard about the opportunity I'm putting in front of you tonight yet." Devon was getting the sinking feeling that she and Mel weren't here for the same reasons.

"Out of curiosity, what is it that you think we're here for?" Devon asked, growing more puzzled and suspicious by the moment.

"Don't be silly, you're here so that I can tell you about the amazing business opportunity that I've just become a part of." Devon quieted her urge to groan out loud.

"Have you ever wished you could get rid of dry cracking skin..." Mel began her pitch and Devon immediately tuned out. When the food was delivered, she asked the server to go ahead and bring her check. She noted that Mel hadn't ordered any food. Devon ordered a beer, hoping to make the time pass quicker. As the server brought a tray holding the beer Mel suddenly swung her arm upward in a gesture of victory. The tray and the beer both fell on top of Devon. She looked down at her now drenched blouse. A brand new top which she had convinced herself to splurge on, in hopes there would be a special occasion fit to wear it.

"Oh, no! I'm so sorry, let me help you." Their server said, a genuine grimace on his face.

"That's okay. I think I'm just going to pay my bill and get out of here." Devon said. Her mood as ruined as her blouse likely was.

"You can't leave yet. I was just about to tell you about our distributor program." Devon waved her off. If nothing else the spilled beer gave her the opportunity to skedaddle without feeling rude. If she hurried she could still fit in a few episodes of *That's My Vacation Home.* She stood, giving Mel a quick goodbye before striding to the front.

The card reader refused to run the first card that she presented. It wasn't until card number three that she was successful. Devon didn't know much about hexes or curses, but this past year she'd studied up. Three seemed to be a significant number. Both bad and good things happened in threes. She stepped outside, the cool October breeze played with her hair.

Walking down the street the heel of her shoe suddenly lodged in a storm grate. Devon pitched forward as the heel separated from her shoe. She fell shoulder first into a puddle on the sidewalk, further ruining her blouse. That would teach her to invest in nice things. An angry moan escaped her lips as she pushed herself to her feet. The drink, the card, and now her heel all added up to three. Hopefully, that meant that she would make it back home and be able to spend the rest of her night in relative peace.

Once home she changed into her pink flannel pajamas and turned on her electric fireplace. On the plus side it wasn't even 10 p.m., giving her plenty of time to watch favorite shows. Devon liked her home, it was cozy and comfortable. She had spent many of her formative years in Nightshade. After high school she had left, and in the time since she'd lived many places. She had spent significant time living in Japan, New York, and Boston.

Last year as her father's health continued to decline as the stress of his job increased, her mother had convinced him to retire. They had put the family home on the market, bought an RV and hadn't looked back. Devon had come to help with the sale of the home. Something about being back had felt right, and on her trip all the stars had aligned. Devon's brother Jamie lived in Nightshade. She had run into her former best friend from high school who had told her about an open position teaching in the Psychology department of Nightshade University. Plus, she had run into her ex-boyfriend who was now a real estate agent. Devon had been accepted for the open position and found a cute home to rent. She had moved there feeling as though everything was meant to be, but one month after moving she'd received a letter. An ominous note claiming someone had put a hex on her was left on her car window one morning.

At first she had been creeped out, then the whole thing had made her laugh. Then her luck took a strange unexpected turn towards the worse. Spilled drinks, unexpected falls, and broken chairs had become commonplace to Devon over the course of the year.

A buzz from her cell made her jump, a look at the screen told her it was her brother Jamie.

"Hey, sis, just wanted to see how the date went?" In response Devon growled into the phone.

"It wasn't a date." She finally said, embarrassment creeping inside her.

"I'm sorry it didn't go well." Her brother's tone was laced with sincerity. Of all the people in her life, her brother understood the pitfalls of being single in a somewhat small town.

"It didn't go at all. I meant seriously it wasn't a date. She wanted to recruit me for her MLM."

"Ouch." Jamie said, tone hushed.

"Yeah. Of course that was in addition to a tray of beer spilling on me, my card not working, and my heel breaking on the way home. The curse strikes again."

"Listen, sis, why don't you let me talk to my friend Em for you."

"Em from high school? Why would you ask her about my string of bad luck?"

"Okay, so, you've been gone awhile but Em kind of came out after highschool."

"Good for her. I sort of wondered but it's not my place to speculate. But how does this help me? I'm cursed, Jamie, I doubt a date with Em is going to fix that."

"Umm, no, sorry. Not that coming out. Although she is gay. What I meant was that technically she's a psychic. She's also really smart. I think maybe she could help you with this hex, or at least point you in a direction." Devon gave a frustrated sigh over the phone. She could almost see her brother smiling on the other end. Jamie continued, voice calm.

"Maybe she knows how to break a curse. At this point do you have anything to lose?" Devon glanced at her very ruined top thrown in the corner. She absolutely didn't have anything to lose and she knew it.

"Okay, I'm game. Give her a call."

"Great, I really think the two of you might like each other."

"I liked her in high school. It's just. Well, you know. We ran in different circles."

"I know. You guys did always get along. She's single, you know?"

"Ugh, Jamie. I've decided dating isn't worth it. I'm just going to die alone on my couch watching my favorite TV shows."

"Ugh, fine. So boring. Did you sign up for the MLM?"

"Jamie!"

"Just asking. I'm sorry you didn't know that's what you were walking into. That sucks."

They spoke for a few more minutes, reviewing one another's day. Devon hung up the phone and sunk into her couch. She flicked the TV back on and settled in, hellbent on enjoying what bit of the night remained.

Her thoughts turned to Emilia Thorne. They had known each other in high school, after Devon's family moved to Nightshade. Emilia had been quick witted if not a little shy and awkward. Devon could remember her braces; her long dark hair usually covered her face. Em had struck an instant friendship with her brother. A friendship which seemingly pulled her brother out of the funk he had settled into after moving. She and Em had always been on friendly terms, they just ran in different circles. They hadn't spent much time together away from her brother. Devon had always thought Em was talented and amazing in her own way. Em had been cast in several of their drama productions. Now Em was apparently a psychic. Devon couldn't wait to catch up with Em and hear all about it.

Chapter 2

Emilia looked out of her foggy window. The crisp Fall day was exactly what she needed to set her mood. Gloomy but with a sky full of possibilities. Perhaps most people only saw the rain and shadows outside, but to Emilia this brought an added layer of comfort. She put on her slippers and robe as she walked through her house. The home had been her Aunt's home before her. Her Aunt Malinda had been a robust woman full of warmth and laughter. Emilia had enjoyed spending the majority of holidays at the house on October Lane with her family. The home was a white, two-story in the colonial style located at 1111 October Lane. Emilia found it charming as it connected to so many wonderful memories. It was the first address Emilia had memorized as a child. Even before her own home address.

After Aunt Malinda died five years ago the home was left to her. Emilia had been honored, the older home had been something her aunt was very proud of. Passed on through the generations four times, and always owned by a female family member.

Emilia sat at her dining table. It was a large table that could seat ten people and was made of solid wood. Because it was so heavy the table had remained in the same spot for at least fifty years. There were places that were nicked and worn, but the wood seemed to always remain smooth.

Today Emilia was forcing herself to plan for her annual Halloween party. A tradition she had begun five years ago when she had moved in. The party seemed to grow in size steadily every year, to the point that she didn't know half the people who attended. She realized that the house was the perfect setting for Halloween parties. She tried to host as many things as possible in the Fall. It seemed to her as though her friend's schedules opened up to her more in the Fall. All except her friend Jamie- he was a constant in her life. He along with several others would be coming over that evening for a night of scary movies.

She stared down at her planning notebook. In large letters the words *HALLOWEEN PARTY* stared back at her in orange marker. Below that she had written: *Readings???* Every year she had this dilemma. Her friends and people in general were interested in her psychic abilities. Either because they found the idea outlandish or spooky in some way. Both her aunt and her grandmother had always had incredible intuition, and Emilia was a psychic who had gained some notoriety of her own. That being said, her gifts had never gained her much in the way of friendship. As a child other kids had found her odd, and as an adult the theme had seemed destined to continue. She didn't let it bother her; the friendships Emilia had cultivated were strong. For her having a couple solid friendships and a few good acquaintanceships was more than enough.

Every year she struggled with whether or not to share her gift. Whether or not she should let people into that part of her life. Her phone buzzed in her pocket and Emilia closed her notebook. The screen said Jamie, so she answered. She would always answer for Jamie.

"Hey there." Emilia said.

"Hey, Em, do you have a minute?"

"For you, I have more than a minute. What's up?"

"Do you remember my sister Devon?" That was a ridiculous question. It was impossible to forget a woman like Devon. Beautiful, popular, and constantly at the center of everyone's universe.

"Of course, I remember her. Why? Is she okay?"

"Umm, well... That's a complicated question." Jamie's tone warbled, obviously trying to decide what to say.

"Was she in an accident or something?" Emilia asked, and was a little surprised by the concern creeping into her own voice.

"Not exactly," Jamie said, beginning to sound even more confused.

"Why don't you start at the beginning," Emilia suggested.

"Okay, good idea. So a year ago, Devon got this note in the mail. No return address. All it says is: *I put a hex on you.*"

"That was it?"

"Yeah, we laughed it off at first because it seemed so ridiculous. But it's been a year and her luck hasn't been the same since."

"Hhmm, I see."

"Could I bring her to movie night for you to talk to?" Jamie asked. Emilia's heart stopped beating. What on earth was she going to have to say to Devon Willis? Just being around her made Emilia uncomfortable. Devon was pretty and intelligent, and the kind of nice baked into a Disney princess. In short Devon was everything that Emilia was not.

"Sure. I don't know exactly what you want me to do. You

realize I don't curse people right?"

"Of course, I know that. It's just you know more about this stuff then we do. Maybe you could help her come up with a solution." Jamie said with so much hope in his voice that Emilia couldn't bear to squash it.

"So you want me to help break a hex that was put on your sister?"

"Yes," Jamie said sheepishly. Then added.

"I know how all this sounds."

"It's okay, Jamie. I'm happy to talk to her. Just swing by with her tonight."

"Seriously, thank you so much! You're really helping me out. I had no idea what to do." Emilia didn't want to tell Jamie that she had no idea how to help his sister. There were a lot of variables in hexes and curses. The two spoke for a few minutes before hanging up. Emilia took a moment to let what had just happened wash over her. Fucking Devon Willis was coming to her house tonight. A girl so full of sunshine and glitter it was like watching an internet video of puppies in a basket while being sprinkled with golden glitter. Emilia gave a long sigh plopping her head against the table.

She and Devon had really only spoken a handful of times. In high school Devon had been the head cheerleader. Where most of the popular kids would make fun of her or ignore her, Devon was always kind. And even though she would never admit it to Jamie, Devon had been her first official girl crush. A red heat spread into her cheeks and she knew she was blushing. Emilia wanted to call Jamie back and cancel, but she would never do that. Tonight, Devon would be in her home, the thought of it made her heart speed, but not in an altogether unpleasant way. She was an adult, surely spending a little face time with Devon Willis wouldn't break her.

Chapter 3

Devon stared blankly into her closet, unsure what to wear. Her brother had told her it wasn't a costume party, but to be cute. She finally decided on a cute dress she had gotten for Halloween the previous year. The dress was a deep purple with silver moons and stars all over it. She fluffed out her long auburn hair, letting it hang over her shoulders. The doorbell rang and she screamed instead of opening it.

"Come on in. I'll be out in a few minutes." She heard the door open and the sound of Jamie rifling through her fridge a moment later. She finished putting in her crescent moon earrings before coming out.

"You know, I can't believe you just let me in here. I could have been some serial killer."

"But you're not."

"But what if I had been?"

"Then I guess I wouldn't have to worry about talking to

some girl about breaking my recent string of bad luck." Jamie groaned and rolled his eyes.

"You're incorrigible, you know that?"

"Yes, and you love me for it."

They arrived at Emilia's home exactly on time. Jamie was punctual to a fault. Devon took a minute to examine the house. The large colonial home should have seemed imposing but there was something warm and welcoming about it. The place instantly gave Devon good vibes. They walked inside and the whole house smelled like cinnamon and apple cider.

"This place is amazing," Devon whispered to Jamie.

"I know, it's a really fun place. I'm going to go find Em."

"Don't rush her, I know she's in the middle of hostessing."

"Seriously, it's fine. She's expecting you." Devon was about to admonish her brother yet again when he pointed to the top of the stairs.

"Oh look, there she is now." Jamie waved his arms in the air to get Emilia's attention. She saw Jamie first, then for the briefest moment she locked eyes with Devon. Emilia broke eye contact almost immediately, but in that moment Devon took in the full sight of her.

As Emilia came down the stairs Devon had to hold back a gasp. Gone was the scrawny girl who was all knees and elbows. In the years since she'd seen her last Emilia had grown into herself. She stood at the top of the stairs perfectly backlit by purple Halloween lights. Her black hair fell in a perfect wave of curls along her shoulders. She wore a dress which was orange with black cats, along with a pair of black leggings. The outfit hugged her in all the right places showing off her curves.

As she approached Emilia locked eyes with Devon, and this time she didn't look away. Emilia's eyes were the most perfect shade of emerald green and held inside them a warm gentleness. The sight of her took Devon's breath. Gone was her baby brother's little friend and in her place was this new Emilia, who had an almost ethereal beauty. The sight of her was such a shock to the system that it took her brother elbowing her in the side to bring her back. She realized that Emilia had been talking to her.

"Oh, I'm sorry. I was admiring how you've got the place set up. I really dig it."

"Thank you, I was afraid maybe I overdid it this year with the decorations."

"No, I think it's perfect," Devon said, giving the place another scan. If she wasn't mistaken when she turned back around, she caught Emilia checking her out as well. A surprising sense of excitement sprang to life deep inside her.

"She's right, Em, the place looks amazing." Devon remembered for the first time that her brother was standing beside them. A glance at Emilia's face seemed to indicate she was having a similar reaction. Emilia reached out her arms hugging Jamie.

"Thanks, it makes me feel better when I know you like something. That usually means other people are going to like it too," Emilia said to Jamie, who was already looking distracted.

"I'm sorry but are you watching *Practical Magic* in there?" Jamie asked.

"Of course. You know it's the first movie I put on every Halloween." Jamie nodded his head. Devon internally congratulated Emilia for having good taste.

"Hey, you two are good to talk this hex thing out, right?" Jamie asked, an urgent plea in his tone.

"Sure, Jamie, just go and abandon us. It's fine," Devon said with a smirk.

"Thanks, sis," Jamie said, ignoring the smirk and running off to watch the movie.

"He loves that movie, insists that we watch it every year."

"I can't say that I blame him. It's a great movie," Devon said.

"You like *Practical Magic*?" The surprise in Emilia's tone made Devon laugh.

"Who do you think introduced Jamie to it?" Devon said with a sweet smile.

"You've got me there," Emilia said. She paused, seeming to scan the room then returning her gaze to Devon.

"It's pretty crowded down here, you want to go talk in my room?" Emilia asked. Devon felt her heart pick up speed, beating faster against her chest.

"Yeah, that sounds great," Devon answered. She followed Emilia up the stairs, allowing her eyes to linger longer than necessary on the woman's figure as she climbed. Emilia walked through the first door on the right and Devon followed. The room was clearly Emilia's bedroom. For a moment, Devon felt like she was in high school again visiting a crush's home for the first time. The room had off the charts good vibes. Potted plants filled much of the space, sitting on the floor or hanging from the ceiling. There were various rocks, crystals, and gemstones decorating a bookshelf and her bedside table. Devon bent down to examine a brightly colored one.

"That's Fluorite," The casualness of Emilia's tone set Devon at ease.

"I like it. You seem to have a lot of rocks."

"Geology has always been an interest of mine, and plants. I've always enjoyed studying the natural world around me. I guess through the years my collection grew."

"Did you ever study it, like in college or school?" Devon didn't like the way the question sounded in her ears. She sounded like a freshman asking her first big girl college question.

"I took as many college courses in the sciences as I could. But at the end of the day it's mostly a hobby. I love learning for its own sake."

"I think that's really cool. I wish I had something I enjoyed enough that I wanted to be studious about it."

"What did you end up doing? Career wise?"

"I went the psychology route. I teach a few courses at the local college, and I work pretty closely with the recruitment office."

"I think psychology counts as a cool thing to be studious about." Emilia said with a smile.

"I guess you're right. I'm used to people not taking it very seriously."

"I mean you're talking to a psychic in Nightshade, so I can relate to not being taken seriously." Devon hadn't considered that a misunderstanding of their professions would be something they had in common. Emilia unfolded a small table and pulled up two chairs. In her hands she held what appeared to be a deck of cards. Emilia sat on one chair and gestured for Devon to take the other. As she sat she watched Emilia cut the deck of cards. Looking closer, Devon realized the deck was of Tarot cards.

"So, Jamie says you're a psychic. I apologize but I'm a little unfamiliar with all that encompasses," Devon said, her nerves began to kick in. The last thing she wanted to do was insult the woman in front of her, but it also occurred to her that she was clueless as to what she had just signed up for."

"That's okay, most people don't know much about it. I like

to start with a definition because I find it helps people stress out less. So, I'm a psychic. Put simply, I make predictions and inferences about the future based on my intuition."

"I thought everyone had intuition," Devon said, her tone neutral.

"Yes, on some level I believe everyone does, a psychic just has a clearer ability to predict the future." Devon felt her body relax, dissecting something into parts was the natural way her brain worked.

"So, do you also get messages from dead people?" Devon asked. Emilia gave the deck one more shuffle before stopping and holding the cards in her hands.

"No, that's a medium."

"There's a difference?"

"There is. A medium is someone who can communicate with those who have died. They get messages from the dead and that gives them insights into people's lives. All mediums are psychic, not all psychics are mediums." Emilia explained with the ease of someone who has had the same conversation dozens of times. Devon nodded her head, taking everything in.

"You're a psychic, but do you do anything else? What I

mean, is this what you do for a living or do you fill your days with something else as well?"

"I do. I opened a store called Natural Wonders about three years ago."

"Ahh, so you have found a way to do something with your hobbies." Devon felt a warm smile cross her face.

"Life gets dull if you can't surround yourself with the things you love and appreciate." Em lifted her eyes meeting Devon's. She found an unexpected jolt of electricity go through her.

"I think you might be right about that."

"So, rumor has it, that you have a bit of a hex problem," Emilia said, making the leap to get down to business.

"It would seem so," Devon said with a shrug.

"Did you bring the original note you received?"

"I did, Jamie said it might be able to tell you something about the original intention for the hex. But it's been over a year, I'm not sure what the paper is going to be able to tell you." Devon pulled out a crumpled piece of paper. She unfolded it, placing it on the table in front of Emilia.

"I certainly make no promises, but maybe we'll both be surprised." Emilia said with a grin. She watched as Emilia sat holding the paper in her hands, studying the writing first then the paper itself. Emilia placed the note back on the table and began shuffling the deck of cards. Within seconds a card seemingly flew from the deck. Emilia placed the card face up in front of the note.

"Were you dating a lot in the time right before you got this note?" Emilia asked.

"Umm actually, yeah. I guess so. I was trying to open myself up more," Devon said. Emilia nodded her head. She continued shuffling the deck, another card jumped from the deck and was placed beside the first card.

"Did you meet up with any people from your past around that time?"

"Actually yeah, I came back into town to sell my parents' home. They retired last year. I met up with a bunch of people I used to know. Em nodded again. She continued shuffling, watching as one more card fell from the deck.

"I don't think this person wanted to hurt you. Just inflict you with petty inconveniences. Does that sound accurate?" Em asked.

"Yeah, nothing dangerous has happened." Devon cocked her head to one side, taking in the whole of the experience.

"I think maybe I can help you. Meet me at my store tomorrow morning."

"Your store? Do rocks break curses?"

"No, but hopefully they can increase your luck. And if not, they'll be pretty to look at while we check out my more witchy section." Emilia gave her a smirk.

"Right. That probably makes more sense," Devon said with a smile of her own.

"Thanks, Emilia." Devon couldn't see her own face but she knew her smile was wide and genuine."

"Call me Em."

"Alright. Thanks, Em. I guess being a psychic must make you pretty popular around Halloween time."

"Only when I'm breaking hexes," Em said her voice taking on a hint of snark. Devon had inadvertently hit a nerve, it was clear on Em's face.

"I didn't mean that in a rude way," Devon said, keeping her tone as light as possible. She watched as the tension in Em's face eased.

"I know, I'm sorry. It's just people in my life, friends... They tend to come to you when you're a psychic. When you have good news to tell them it's all rainbows and butterflies. This is my friend Em. She's an amazing psychic. But as soon as you tell them something not great, suddenly you're not so welcome anymore. Truthfully, I've moved away from giving readings. I mostly stick to running the store these days. Jamie asked me to look into your problem, and, well, I can't say no to Jamie." Em said, there was a far off look in her eyes, and Devon suspected she had brought up something unexpectedly painful.

"That does sound rough. I'm happy for whatever help you can give me. For what it's worth, I have a hard time saying no to my brother as well," Devon met Em's eyes. Em smiled.

"Thanks, I needed that," Em said.

"So tomorrow, around 10 a.m. work for you?" Devon asked with a shrug of her shoulders.

"That's perfect. Let's see if we can't get you some luck back," Em rose and walked towards the door. Devon took the hint and followed. She gave the room with its rocks and plants one more look before turning to go. Devon couldn't help thinking how well the night had gone so far. As soon as the thought entered her mind she cursed it internally. Her eyes trained on Em, she went to take the first step downstairs and missed. She was going to fall ass over head down the stairs. Except she didn't. Em reached a hand back, steadying her before she could fall. Devon cautiously drew in a breath. Em turned, meeting her eyes. Devon tried to give an apologetic smile, but Em waved her off.

"I guess I should have expected something like that, what with all this talk about curses." Em chuckled.

"Em, I'm so sorry. Are you hurt?" Devon asked, concern etched her voice.

"Me? I'm fine. Are you alright?" Em asked scanning Devon for any apparent injuries.

"I'm fine. You get used to falling after a year of being hexed, but I wasn't prepared to be caught midfall. Good catch." Devon offered a smile.

"I'm glad I could help," Em said.

"Are you ladies alright?" Jamie asked from the bottom of

the stairs.

"We're fine, Jamie, just showing Em my curse up close."

"Goodness, couldn't get a night off, huh?" Jamie asked, trying to tease and falling woefully short of funny. Devon's face fell a little.

"Hey, everything is going to be okay. Nothing is broken. We'll meet up tomorrow and figure this thing out," Em said rubbing Devon's arm. Devon glanced down at Em's hand just as she pulled it away. The gesture was warm and comforting. Devon felt a tinge of heat rising up her neck.

"I hope you're right," Devon said, with her best forced laugh.

"Of course I'm right. I am a psychic after all," Em teased, with a wink. The joke made Devon feel far less lonely. Once she was assured one more time that Em was uninjured she had Jamie take her home. Jamie was slightly angry that he had to leave before *Practical Magic* ended, but he complied. Tomorrow was a new day...and hopefully by the end of it Devon would have her luck back.

Chapter 4

Em wrestled with her blankets. The night with Devon had not been at all what she had expected. For one, wasn't there some kind of rule against being beautiful, smart, and funny? Didn't people only get one out of the three, maybe two if they were very lucky. Yet, there Devon had been with her gorgeous red hair, perfect body and being just as witty as Em remembered her being in high school.

Em hadn't expected Devon to take a second glance at her. But she could swear she'd caught Devon checking her out more than once. Em guessed it was flattering, after all Devon was easily a ten. Or well, a ten if one didn't take the whole being cursed thing into account. That definitely did put a damper on Devon's shine. Though if she was honest, having an excuse to spend time with Devon hadn't been all together unpleasant.

I'm definitely going to have to up my game tomorrow, Em thought to herself. She had gone into the night swearing that she wouldn't offer to help. Em had told herself that she would point Devon in a basic direction and then remove herself from the situation. But one look in those warm hazel eyes and Em had felt herself give. Em gave one more aggravated flop over to her other side before giving up. She sat up and grabbed her phone. Em typed "how to break a curse" in her search bar. The results were mostly unhelpful. There were people she could call. Lovely people who she knew that ascribed to spell work. She sighed and sent an email to one of them. The pull of sleep seemed to be dragging her. Em put her phone on the charger and allowed her eyes to close.

The terrible whine of her alarm clock ripped her awake the next morning. Em stretched out her arms and legs with a yawn. She checked her phone and was happy to see a reply email sent by Gail Merristrom. She had met Gail years ago during a protest to save a grove of trees in downtown Nightshade. The tree grove had been there for hundreds of years, but the town council approved a plan to cut them down. All so some land developer could build apartment buildings. Em and Gail had bonded right away. Gail tended towards the witchy end of the spiritual and Em was happy to have her input. She detailed several ways one might go about halting a hex. Em had always found spell work fascinating. Personally, she preferred to remain undefined as far as her spiritual preferences went. She respected everyone.

Em drank her coffee letting her thoughts drift. The

sudden buzz of her cell snapped her back into focus. She checked and saw a message from Devon.

"We still on for this morning?"

"Of course, I have my bag of tricks all ready." Em smiled as she sent the message.

"Wait. Just so I'm clear this is a hypothetical bag of tricks right?" Devon's response came before Em had a chance to lay her phone down.

"Nope, it's a real bag."

"Em I can't tell if you're being serious."

"It's just like Mary Poppins bag, or the Tardis. It's bigger on the inside." Something about lightly teasing Devon made her heart thud a little louder, she could hear it in her ears.

"Oh. You're very funny. Very cute." Devon's reply came quickly and Emilia found herself staring at the word cute. It had to be a typo or an autocorrect. There was no way that her high school crush had just called her cute. Emilia stared at her reflection in the hallway mirror. She had grown up, definitely maturing into herself. Her confidence in who she was solidified, but she wouldn't have thought someone like Devon would notice her. Emilia shook her head. She looked down at her phone

and decided not to text back, Devon would meet her at the store in a few minutes.

One benefit to living one street away from downtown was that Emilia was always close to work. Her store, Natural Wonders, had been a dream of hers for a very long time. She and her Aunt had talked about it for years. When her aunt had died Em was her sole heir. She had received the house and a note. The letter from her aunt had encouraged her to use the money left to her to finally open the store. So she had. Natural Wonders was born from grief and love. The store was everything she had imagined. It wasn't large or trendy, but it was hers. In the back room she offered psychic readings three days a week. She had developed a good reputation within the community and people sometimes traveled to come see her.

Today the store was a welcome sight. She was surprised to find Devon standing outside waiting for her.

"You're early," Em said.

"I stopped and got us coffee, and usually I spill it. Or sometimes I fall. Usually I'm delayed in some way."

"You're rambling," Em said, lips quirking into a smile.

"I am. It's just that I'm... Well, I'm sorry if earlier when

I called you cute I crossed some kind of line. You might not be single, but I didn't mean it in a creepy way," Devon said, her words came in a string so long Em wondered how she managed not to stop for a breath.

"I didn't take it in a creepy way. It's nice that you think I'm cute. I just didn't want to assume anything." Em took the coffee and walked inside, ushering Devon to follow. Internally she waged a war. She should tell Devon that she was cute too. Before she could say anything she got an intuitive nudge. She turned in time to see Devon tripping over the entryway. Em's hands reached out, catching her midfall. Her coffee was a casualty but Devon's bones were safe. She helped set Devon upright and stared into her deep eyes.

"Oh, my goodness, is she okay?" A voice from inside the store asked. Em turned and saw Violet, her store manager, rushing towards them.

"I'm fine, nothing is hurt but my pride." Em felt a twinge of sympathy for the woman.

"I'll run and get the carpet cleaner." Em said heading towards the storage closet. She could hear Devon explaining the hex to Violet. When Em came back with the cleaner Violet had a necklace out, showing it to Devon. Em shook her head unsure what hijinks Violet was up to. Violet was an older woman of sixty and then some. She was short and squat with hair that was so white Em was sure it couldn't be natural. Her eyes were blue and misted a bit from age, but she had within them a keen look. Em enjoyed working with the older woman, for her good humor among other things.

"Em, did you know that Violet has found the perfect thing for me?"

"Oh, has she?" Em asked shooting Violet a glance as she bent to clean the coffee now soaking into the carpet.

"Yes, she just happens to have an amulet that repels hexes on hand." Devon sounded so hopeful that Em was almost inclined to go along with the charade. There was something to the science of placebos after all.

"Seriously, Violet?" Em said, shooting her a look.

"What? I was just being helpful," the old woman said in her most soothing voice.

"Devon, no. She's just messing with you. That's a necklace we bought in bulk. It's made in China," Em said, shooting Violet a stern glance. Violet rolled her eyes and continued her work behind the counter. Devon turned the necklace over, saw the sticker and immediately burst into loud laughter.

"Oh, my gosh. I was totally going to buy that thing. I guess I was lucky you were watching out for me." The words were spoken without any grand meaning behind them. But they struck Emilia all the same.

"Well, of course I'm here to look out for you. I can't have people getting swindled at my store." She and Devon both laughed.

"Out of curiosity what do you think is the best way to proceed when it comes to getting my luck back?"

"I think what would be best is some protection and reversal magic. I have a few things in the store that can help with the luck part. I'll get everything together and I think we should get together tonight during the new moon."

"Sounds great. You want me to meet at your place?" Devon asked.

"Umm, yeah, that sounds like a great idea."

"I don't suppose you'd want to meet me for dinner first?"

"I might be persuaded. Girl has to eat," Em said coyly. Devon gave a chuckle.

"Hmm, I've got to get going. My first class starts in thirty minutes. But why don't you meet me at Shabu in town. Say around 6:30?" Devon asked.

"Sounds great." Emilia said, her eyes meeting Devon's in a smoldering stare. Em held the contact for as long as she could. Devon blushed a shade of pink then headed for the door. She turned back to Em before exiting.

"Thanks again, Em. For helping me out." Devon said, her tone brimming with sincerity.

"Of course. I'm happy to help." Em watched as Devon left, the all too familiar pang of loneliness filled her. She had a carefully curated life in Nightshade. Filled with people that were a part of her life without being painfully close. Except for Jamie, who had unwittingly snuck through the cracks in her walls. Emilia wondered if Devon might be slipping through her walls too? All she knew for certain was that when the woman was with her it brought out feelings of excitement long since buried.

"Looks like someone has a date tonight." Violet smirked smugly from behind the counter.

"It's not a date."

"It's dinner with a beautiful woman. A dinner that said

beautiful woman invited you to."

"Not a date."

"It's totally a date."

"Violet, come on. Look at her, she's easily a ten. And I'm a…" Em forced herself to cut off.

"Also easily a ten, don't sell yourself short." Em felt a blush rise in her cheeks. She felt good about her looks. But in her mind Devon still felt like the unattainable homecoming queen.

"Thank you, that's sweet of you to say. It's just Devon and I are still very different. She's a lecturer at the college, and I run a store on the square."

"Something tells me she sees you as more than that."

"Still not a date." Em repeated as she walked down the hallway to her office. She shut the door behind her and sank into her chair. Was she going on a date with Devon later? Or was this a dinner between two new friends? Em closed her eyes and told herself she would accept either option.

Chapter 5

Devon ran all the way from the parking lot to her lecture hall. When she stumbled into her room she was out of breath. She had been caught off guard by a sudden rainstorm that seemed to follow her from Emilia's store all the way back to campus. The sudden clearing of a throat caused her to startle and turn around. Stuart Berns sat legs outstretched crossed at the ankles in her chair.

"Stuart, do I have the wrong lecture hall?" Devon asked.

"No, I was waiting for you." Devon looked the man up and down. She had dated men in the past and even connected with a couple of them. Stuart was not a man she wanted to feel more of a connection to. He was older than her by about ten years, graying and balding in an unattractive way. Above everything else, Devon found him to be trendy in a pretentious way. He was the sort of man who wore glasses without a prescription because they gave the appearance of intelligence.

"Oh, what can I do for you?" Devon said, keeping one eye

on Stuart as she readied herself for class.

"Well, the school is having its annual Fall Festival and I was hoping you would go with me." Devon's heart sank, she had no interest in being Stuart's plus one to any function.

"Ahh, I'll definitely see you there." She hadn't answered the question exactly to the man's liking, it was clearly written across his face.

"I was hoping we could go together, like on a date." Stuart persisted. Devon didn't know what she had done to insinuate to Stuart that she would want to go on a date. Torn between not wanting to hurt his feelings, and not appreciating his timing or delivery Devon thought quickly.

"I'm actually already seeing someone," Devon lied.

"Really? I was under the impression that your date with Mel went poorly." There was a look of genuine confusion on Stuart's face. It was good to know that all of her colleagues knew about her shitty dating life already.

"It isn't Mel." Devon quipped trying to appear busy behind her podium.

"Who is it?" Stuart asked.

"Her name is Emilia." Devon said. She immediately regretted the words. The moment was spiraling out of control and Devon felt it.

"Oh, well then. I guess I've waited too long to ask for the second time." Stuart said, his tone serious. Maybe that was why she couldn't see herself dating him. He was far too serious.

"Yes, but as I said I'm sure we'll see each other there. Oh, my class is getting ready to start," Devon said. She still had fifteen minutes, but she had a routine she enjoyed going through during that time. Stuart, who appreciated routine, understood her meaning. He gave a sad little wave as he left her room. Devon knew she should feel bad, but all she felt was relief. It was a problem within herself that she felt bad saying no to people. Of course now she had to tell Em what had happened, extend an invitation and hope that she said yes.

Devon's lecture went without a hitch. Of course, she had given the lecture on attending titled, "What our brains think is important" about a thousand times. Still, ever since her run of bad luck started she didn't take things going smoothly for granted. Devon was grateful she only had the one class to teach today. She went home and took a long much needed bath. One of the things she had loved about the older home she rented was the clawfoot tub.

Devon still hadn't worked out whether her dinner with Emilia tonight was meant to be a date. She had asked, and Em accepted. Devon was inclined towards letting the dinner and the night be whatever it turned into organically. Emilia was beautiful, intelligent, and charming. It would be a lie to say that she wasn't attracted to Em. But since moving back to Nightshade Devon couldn't deny her own loneliness. She realized that her friendships were scattered throughout the world, but none were here in the place she currently lived. Whatever she felt with Em would sort itself out. If at the end of the day what she ended up with was a new friendship, that was more than enough.

Shabu was by far Devon's favorite restaurant in Nightshade. Styled as an all-you-can-eat Japanese hot pot. Devon had developed a habit of going once a week for the delicious soups she could make from the ingredients provided for her.

Inside, Em was waiting for her. She wore a black shirt that fitted her perfectly and a skirt that flowed out from her. The skirt was a deep purple with the constellations and planets emblazoned across it. Em's long dark hair was pulled back from her face. Devon stood there studying the woman for a moment. The sight of her took Devon's breath away. She looked down at her own outfit, jeans, a gray shirt and flats. Devon gave herself points because the shirt and the jeans fit her well.

Em turned and saw her, breaking the spell. She waved enthusiastically when she saw Devon. Her reaction made Devon's stomach do flips inside her. Em walked over and gave her a hug. Devon's stomach went from doing flips to a full-blown gymnastics routine. A server approached and took them to their table.

"Have you ever been here before?" Devon asked.

"Nope. I'm a first timer. Be gentle with me," Em said teasingly. Devon gulped audibly, as her core grew tight.

"I'm happy to show you the ropes," Devon said with a smirk regaining her confidence. Em gave a nod and a smile.

"Okay, so first you choose your soup broth. Then you go to the buffet and pick your meat that's going to go in the soup. The conveyor belt running by the tables has vegetables and noodles you can throw in."

"Wow, this whole setup is really cool."

"I know, this place reminds me of living in Japan."

"You lived in Japan?"

"Oh yeah, I mean it was only for a little while after school,"

Devon said, downplaying. She remembered all the friends who had written off the experience. All the people from her life who hadn't wanted to hear the details.

"I think that's really cool. How long were you there?" Devon's eyebrows lifted, surprised by the followup question.

"Umm, I was there for three years about five years ago."

"I can't believe Jamie didn't say anything. Then again, that's when my aunt was so sick. I guess he didn't want to bring up too much family stuff."

"Your Aunt Malinda? I didn't realize she was sick." Em arched an eyebrow surprised.

"Umm, she died not long after that. I didn't realize you knew her."

"She did a tarot reading for me before I left for college." Devon noticed Em's eyebrow rise a fraction higher and continued.

"I was dating Brent Turner at the time. The football player. Anyway, I got accepted into my dream university and Brent didn't. He felt really threatened by me going away and he wanted me to stay. I went to your aunt to see what I should do."

"What did she say?"

"The cards showed a pretty bleak future if I stayed in town. I was a little devastated. Brent was my first love. Your aunt told me that if someone being with me was dependent on me sacrificing my dreams then I needed to look at that relationship. So I left, and Brent found a girl his first semester at school. He dumped me for her."

"Sounds like you had lessons to learn outside of town. A whole life to live."

"I did always feel like I needed to stretch my wings."

"What brought you back?"

"I came back to help sell my parents' home. Being back just felt right. The job situation worked out and here I am. Of course, then I was hexed. All this bad luck, has put a damper on moving back." Em gave a smile and nodded.

"I think maybe you were just meant to come back here for a while."

"Could be. It hasn't been all bad. I get to see Jamie more, and I met you." Devon raised her gaze, locking with Em's endlessly green eyes. She could swear she saw a blush light up

Em's face.

"Oh, yes, I'm sure meeting me is the highlight of the year," Em said, in a self-deprecating tone.

"I think it might be. I think you're one of the most interesting people I've ever met."

"Interesting, huh? Is that code for weird?" Em asked, her tone teasing.

"Weird isn't the word I would have chosen. In this case, interesting meant that you're intelligent. You see the world in a very different way than I do, and I enjoy glimpsing things from your perspective." Em's eyebrows raised. She obviously hadn't been expecting the answer. Devon knew she should back away. She knew that she shouldn't push any farther. But there was more she wanted to say.

"Hey, Em," Devon said lightly.

"Yeah." Em responded, her eyes catching and locking onto Devon's.

"I didn't mean weird, but I like weird. I'm honestly about as weird as they come. So, I feel most at home with people that aren't completely 100% normal." Devon shot Em a shy smile. Em tucked a strand of dark hair behind an ear then smiled back.

"I don't think you're awkward."

"Seriously? Because we're going back to your place to un-hex me. That's pretty awkward." Em burst into laughter, catching herself before spitting her drink.

"You have a point," Em said between giggles. She regained her composure before she continued.

"Have you met up with any of your friends from high school?" Em asked. Devon nodded her head.

"Jessica and I both work at the university and Brent was actually my real estate agent. But that's about it. I have a few friends that I've made at the university. I guess you could say my circle is pretty small these days. You and Jamie are kind of it right now, as far as significant hangouts go." Em looked surprised. In high school, Devon had a large social circle. They had felt like real friendships. After graduation they had all scattered to the winds. Devon knew now that they were friendships born from convenience.

"So it really has been just me and Jamie since you moved back?"

"Unless you count Mel, " Devon shrugged her shoulders.

"Who is Mel?" Em asked.

"She's from work. I thought we had a connection. It's funny, I actually thought we went out on a date." Devon began.

"You thought it was a date... but it was...?"

"An MLM presentation. She wanted me to be a part of her down line, just not in a sexy way." Em laughed again.

"Oh wow, an MLM date. That sucks."

"Yeah. This unlucky thing is not for the faint of heart," Devon said, she looked down at her plate. Em reached across the table and patted her hand.

"Hey, your unlucky days are almost over," Em said. Devon met her eyes, there was a deep stirring between both of them. She let herself feel the increasing tension resting inside her.

"If I'm honest it's been a little lonely, being here without any friends."

"Well then, it's a good thing you aren't friendless," Em said, a smile forming across her face. Devon's face must have registered confusion because Em gave an exasperated sigh.

"Hello, I'm your friend now. Hence not friendless."

Devon's face broke into a wide grin.

"That may be one of the nicest things anyone has ever said to me."

"Well, don't tell anyone. I have my frightening reputation to hold onto," Em said with a chuckle.

"My lips are sealed," Devon said, grinning. Em took a sip of her wine, smiling at Devon over the rim of her glass. Devon's gaze was drawn to Em's full lips. She wondered what it would be like to kiss her. What would it be like to hold Em's bottom lip in her teeth. The thoughts caught Devon off guard and she gave her head a sudden shake. Her eyes lifted to Emilia's eyes, they drew her in. The restaurant felt hot all of a sudden. Em's smile broadened and she gave a chuckle.

"What's so funny?" Devon asked, cocking her head to the side.

"You're blushing." Em said.

"I don't blush."

"Let me assure you that you do." Devon could feel the redness in her cheeks deepening. Em spoke up before she could make any more futile denials.

"I think it's cute. Looks good on you." Devon felt herself coming undone on the inside. Something about Emilia was getting to her. Devon wasn't sure what it was about the woman that drew her in so completely. All she knew was that she enjoyed the feeling.

Chapter 6

Emilia walked through her front door and did a quick appraisal. Everything seemed to be in order, fit for company. She gathered the supplies obtained earlier in the day. Candles featured heavily and she found herself embracing the aesthetic by turning out her normal lights. To say the way things were proceeding with Devon were unexpected would be putting it mildly.

It was odd running into her old high school crush after all these years. But even stranger was that now with the passage of time Devon seemed equally interested in her. There was a measured voice deep in her head that told her to proceed with caution. Falling for girls like Devon rarely worked out in her favor. What exactly was *a girl like Devon*, anyway? Thus far the woman had broken every stereotype Emilia had set up in her mind. After tonight Devon wouldn't have any other reasons for hanging around. The hex would be broken and Devon would be gone. There was no reason to invite unnecessary heartbreak into her life. No reason to hope for any other outcome. Sometimes she wished her gift worked on demand. But no matter how she tried to see what possibilities the future held, she was getting nothing.

Devon knocked on her door just as she finished lighting the last candle. She gave her living room one more good look around. The room was lit in the warm glow of candlelight.

"The door is open. Come on in." Emilia called out. She heard the door open and Devon appear.

"What if I was a serial killer?" Devon asked with a smirk.

"I guess I would be dead." Emilia chuckled.

"That's a little grim, don't you think?"

"You're right. I'm sure if you were a serial killer you'd just be here for a psychic reading, and not to you know, murder me." Devon tried to hold back her laugh but it came out in a burst anyway. Her laugh was rich and full, a sound that filled the space between them.

"So what happens next?" Devon said, a smile still hanging from her lips.

"First, I'm going to do a little cleansing with some sage."

"Seriously? Burning sage is an actual thing people do?" Em

shook her head and laughed.

"In the community I'm a part of burning sage is the spiritual equivalent to restarting your computer when it's acting funny."

"I'm game, sage me up."

"This is a cleansing, not a football game."

"Right. Sorry. It's hard to know the right energy I'm supposed to be bringing here."

"I didn't say your energy wasn't cute."

"Oh really, you think I have cute energy?"

"Oh come on, surely you knew I had the biggest crush on you when we were in high school."

"Wait! What? No way. You had a crush on me?"

"Of course I did. Who didn't have a crush on you back then? I mean look at you, you're the total package," Em said gesturing to Devon's entire being.

"You're kidding me. Me? I'm the most awkward human I know."

"Pretty sure you aren't as awkward as you're giving

yourself credit for."

"Em, *Schranz* is my favorite kind of music. I'm definitely not cool. I might not even be normal."

"*Schranz*?" Em asked, tilting her head to one side. Utter confusion written across her face.

"Yeah, German Techno Music."

"Oh, of course. How could I not have known what that was? Don't worry, being normal is pretty overrated." Em giggled.

"That's what I'm trying to tell you. I'm not cool."

"Wow, to think you've just been awkwardly undercover this whole time." Em laughed. Devon gave her a glare but ended it with a smile. Em lit the sage bundle she had rolled earlier in the day while still at the shop. The scent filled the air. Em watched as Devon closed her eyes, inhaling deeply. Devon's red hair fell in soft curls around her face and shoulders. For a moment, Em thought about what it would be like to run her hands through it. She shook the thought away. *Definitely not the reason we're here tonight*, she thought to herself.

Next, Em pulled out three tiny bottles and a bag of crystal chips.

"Ooohh, pretty. What are those?" Devon asked.

"These are known to be stones that enhance luck," Em said. Devon gave her a dubious stare.

"You can look them up later if you like. This is Jade, Aventurine, Citrine, and Clear Quartz. They each bring something unique to the table." Em mixed the tiny stone chips together and poured a mix of them in all three bottles. She put tiny corks in the bottles and sealed them with melted pink wax.

"Take these jars. Put one in your home, one in your car, and carry one on your person for at least a month," Em said, handing the jars to Devon. She took the jars and studied them.

"This is it?"

"Well, what were you expecting?"

"I don't know to be honest. Maybe more chanting."

"Chanting?"

"Well, yeah. I don't know."

"I can chant something if you want me to," Em said with a grin.

"Let's see... Bring Devon luck and good fortune, bring

Devon luck and good fortune," Em chanted, broad smile across her face. Devon leaned in, suddenly kissing Em on the lips. Her words left her in a whimper. Who needed words for a moment like this one. Em allowed herself to be taken into the kiss. Devon caught Em's lower lip in her own, giving it a suck. Em's hand found its way to Devon's mass of red hair, allowing it to flow over her fingers. She closed her eyes, letting herself to go even deeper. Devon pulled back. The motion caught Em by surprise, her eyes shot open. Devon sat with a finger pressed to her lips.

"I'm so sorry. I feel like that probably just came out of nowhere for you," Devon said.

"It's okay. Umm, I liked it." Em offered.

"It wasn't too forward?"

"I think you might be overthinking this. We're both adults, you kissed me." Em said as she placed a finger underneath Devon's chin lifting it until their eyes met.

"And I kissed you back," Em finished with a smile. She leaned in. This time her lips brushed against Devon's. When Em pulled away she heard Devon give a tiny moan.

"That was. Wow."

"That was wow."

"Yeah, I stand by that statement."

"So strange. You coming back into my life after all this time. A pleasant surprise to be sure. Of course, I'm sure you'll be going back to your normal life now that I've done what I can about your hex."

"That's the plan," Devon said. Em turned her face, hoping Devon wouldn't catch her disappointment.

"Hey, that doesn't mean I don't want to hangout anymore," Devon reached out a hand to stroke Em's cheek.

"I knew you liked me," Em said with her smile coming back to her face.

"But I like hearing that you want to spend more time with me."

"Actually, I was going to invite you to the University's Fall Festival."

"You're in luck. I love Halloween, and I've been known to attend the occasional festival."

"Good. Can I be honest about something?"

"I hope you always choose honesty when it comes to me. I

find I prefer it to being lied to."

"Right. Well, in the interest of honesty. I may have told a guy from work that I was 'seeing' you. Like in a dating way. Please don't be mad. He asked me out and I panicked." Devon raised her hands up in defense.

"Firstly, I'm honored and not angry. I'm happy to be your fake girlfriend anytime. And secondly, you know you're allowed to just say no if someone asks you on a date and you aren't interested."

"I know that, but it's hard for me. Especially since it's a small campus and he's in the same department." Em nodded her head.

"That makes sense. You're trying to avoid making things weird."

"Exactly."

"Well, either way I'll try to be the best fake date you've ever had."

"Hmm, and what if I wanted to ask you on a real date?"

"You want to know what would happen if you asked me out on a real date?" Em asked, taken aback. Devon shot her a grin.

"Yeah." Devon's fingers spider-walked up Em's arm. Em felt a shiver rush through her body. Her mouth went dry and her head started spinning.

"I think if you want to go out on a real date with me you should ask. I like your chances," Em said, her eyes raised to meet Devon's. She found a lust in Devon's eyes that rivaled her own. One look and she knew she was done for. Devon had pulled her in, and Em could only hope she enjoyed the ride.

Chapter 7

Secretly Devon loved dressing in warm layers. She always had. This was the primary reason that Autumn was her favorite season. Devon appraised her outfit in her bedroom mirror. She wore a yellow sweater with a red scarf. The scarf had more sentimental attachment than functional use. Her grandmother had knitted the scarf for her. Some of her friends in high school had made light jokes about the scarf, until she had explained where it came from. Devon didn't care, she loved it.

Her jeans fit her well and even though it wasn't quite cold enough yet, she wore her boots. She smiled at her reflection in the mirror. Last night had been the best night's rest she'd had in almost a year. The bar of crystal chips sat on her dresser, she looked at it fondly. She wasn't a superstitious person, but she hadn't had any bad luck events since Em gave her the bottles. The psychologist in her needed to be able to dissect that, to analyze the components. Her heart was just grateful something had worked, and it knew better than to look a gift horse in the mouth.

S'more Fest was a Nightshade tradition, the town's version of a Fall festival. Devon hadn't been since high school, but tonight she would be there with Em. *With Em.* There was something about those two words that felt strange and yet undeniably comfortable. They would put that to the test tonight. Jamie would be seeing them together; a minefield Devon wasn't sure she wanted to navigate. Em had always been Jamie's best friend, while she had always been Jamie's sister. What would it mean for the two of them to show up together? She pulled her scarf tighter around her and took a breath.

S'more's Fest was exactly how Devon remembered it, perhaps it had grown since high school. There were tables lined with different kinds of chocolate bars and marshmallows. Graham crackers were an option, but so were cookies, and doughnuts. Devon was startled by a pair of hands reaching around her waist settling against her hips.

"Hey there." Em's voice purred in her ears. Devon's body relaxed, easing into Em's touch.

"Hey, yourself. This is amazing. I think it's doubled in size since the last time I was here."

"Very likely. The mayor has really tried to make it appeal to tourists."

"Oh, yes, Nightshade is known for its tourism," Devon teased.

"It is now." Em shrugged. Devon glanced around, there were plenty of people she'd known for years. On second glance there were many she didn't know.

"Huh, well."

"We're close to Salem. But we're cheaper."

"They should paint that on the town sign."

"I have some paint in my garage. We could just do it for them." Em winked.

"Oh, you're going to get me into trouble." Devon laughed. Em tightened her grip on her waist. Devon sucked in a breath.

"Maybe, but it'll be the best kind of trouble," Em breathed out in a hushed whisper.

"There you two are. I've been looking for you." Jamie's voice was loud over the crowd. Devon sighed as she felt Em release her grip and turn to greet her brother.

"Well, we've been right here," Em said. Devon wished Em would wrap her arms around her again.

"Yep, here we are." The words sounded strange even to her. Jamie just nodded his head.

"Have you shown Devon around yet?" Jamie asked Em.

"I wouldn't dare take your job," Em teased. Before she could protest Jamie grabbed Devon's hand and began leading her around.

She was escorted around the various chocolate tables. Devon took a deep inhale, allowing the scent of chocolate to fully envelop her. Jamie dutifully explained the system of the new and improved S'more's Fest.

"You pay your $5 at the front, they give you a red band. Then you get to make as many s'mores as you want." Jamie finished explaining.

Devon nodded her head. She didn't remember the event being so overwhelming. Em took her by the hands rubbing her thumbs across her knuckles.

"Where do you want to start?" Em asked.

The gesture didn't go unnoticed by Jamie. His eyes opened wide, double their normal size. Jamie pointed at their hands, still folded together. Devon opened her mouth, only to watch her brother turn and march into the crowd.

"Oh shit, is he mad?" Em asked, confused.

"I don't know. Let's go find him."

Finding Jamie didn't take long, he was sitting under a large sugar maple tree. Stacks of hay bales lined the trees and Jamie had taken one to sit on. Devon approached giving his back a scratch.

"Hey, we weren't trying to upset you."

"Upset me? Are you kidding? This is amazing!"

"So you're... happy?" Em asked.

"Of course I'm happy! My sister and my best friend are here, together. My two favorite people...together. I'm going to explode into a puff of glitter and smoke."

"Well, that seems excessive," Em teased.

"Excessive! Excessive. I know no such word. Now, we should all get chocolate before the good stuff is taken," Jamie proclaimed. They began their walk back to the tables. Devon locked arms with Jamie.

"Thanks."

"For what?"

"For being cool, with Em and I being here together."

"Why wouldn't I be cool with it?"

"I was afraid you might be a little upset."

"Ahh. Yeah." Jamie gave a chuckle. They walked in silence for half a moment before Jamie continued.

"You and Em are very important to me. I want you to both be happy, and if you happen to find that together… even better." Jamie gave her arm a squeeze. As they approached the chocolate table Devon heard an all too familiar voice calling her name.

"Devon! Devon, is that you?" She cringed inwardly. Outwardly, she plastered a pleasant expression across her face. Em caught the expression and turned with her to see Brent Claywall approaching. Brent had been her high school sweetheart. She had been convinced that he would be her soulmate. Of course, at eighteen who didn't think every romantic entanglement was their true love? He had wanted her to pass over her out-of-state scholarship. Had asked her to go with him to Nightshade Community College. She had opted to take her scholarship. A semester later they were broken up. In the years since, she had gotten her degrees and traveled, while

Brent had stayed securely rooted to the same spot. The high school quarterback turned town real estate agent. He was still handsome, though his hair was thinning and he'd gained weight around the middle. He still had those piercing blue eyes, and a killer smile.

"I knew that was you. God, how long has it been? A couple years?" Devon held back a groan. Brent knew that the two of them had seen each other last year. She had come to oversee the sale of her parents' home after they retired and moved. Devon had been surprised but not disappointed to find out Brent was the real estate agent. After the sale he had asked her out to celebrate and she had said yes. But when it became apparent that he was only interested in one thing, she had ended the night early.

"I think we saw each other last year. Remember you sold my parents' home," she said with a shrug as she smiled.

"Yeah. Oh, no wait a minute. That's right, how could I have forgotten?" Devon bit back her groan even harder. Em cleared her throat and Devon was glad for the interruption.

"Brent, you remember my brother Jamie. And Emilia Thorne." Brent's smile broadened. Devon thought she saw Em wince.

"Of course, Emilia Thorne. You own the house at 111 October Lane right?" Brent extended his hand which Em begrudgingly took. Devon watched as her expression soured.

"I do. I took it on after my aunt died."

"Of course, that's right. I would love to talk to you about converting the old place to an Airbnb at some point."

"I'm not interested." Em said somewhat curtly, turning to walk away.

"It was nice to see you again Brent. I should get going," Devon said, turning to follow Em. When she caught up to Em she linked their arms. Em stopped, turning to meet her gaze. Em's green eyes shined bright, highlighted by the flames of the bonfires being lit around them.

"Devon, did you see Brent before you got that note last year?"

"Umm, yeah, I guess I did."

"It was him."

"What was him?"

"The hex. It was him."

"How do you know?" Devon asked. Em held up two of her fingers pointing to her temples as she closed her eyes.

"Call it a hunch," Em said with a smirk. Devon disliked how much sense that made.

"But why? After all these years?"

"I got the sense that you made him feel like he had stayed frozen in time. That and I don't think you gave him what he was looking for on that date." Devon blushed. That much was true. Brent had been very forward on their date.

"Don't do it sis, the neanderthal isn't worth it." Jamie said. Devon was already turning to find Brent again. She saw him talking to a young couple with a baby, she took a deep breath and walked over to him. When the young couple with the baby had gone she smacked Brent across the arm.

"Seriously, Brent!"

"Devon, what the hell?"

"Are you the one who sent me that letter and put some weird hex thing on me?" Brent's eyes shifted to see who was around.

"What are you, a teenager? I'm a grown man, I don't put

hexes on people." Devon saw the hint of red creeping up his neck and into his cheeks. She knew then he was lying.

"You liar, it was you!"

"Was not," Brad said, and it reminded Devon of when they were in high school having an argument.

"Oh, come on. You're blushing, and you only do that when you lie."

"Okay, okay. So what? I put a *hex* on you. It's not like they're real. A friend of mine thought it would be funny. We used a book from the farmer's market, for crying out loud."

"Ugh, you're such a child," Devon said angrily as she stormed off for the second time. Brent yelled something about her *overreacting*, but she ignored him. She returned to where her brother and Em stood, a plate ready to make s'mores in her hands.

"What did he say?" Em asked.

"You were right. He admitted it."

"I'm sorry," Em said, reaching out to rub her arm.

"No, it's fine. At least now I know." Jamie gave her a hug before bounding away towards the marshmallow stand.

"Okay, seriously, how did you know it was him?" Devon asked.

"I already told you how." Em said, again pointing to her temples.

"Sure. I know. But like, how does that work?"

"Hmm, that's a good question."

"You don't know the answer?"

"I don't know the science of it all. I guess the best way to explain it is an intuitive nudge. Sometimes I just know things."

"That's going to be a lot for me to unpack."

"If you want my advice, don't try too hard to figure it out."

"Right, I'm never going to think about that again," Devon said with a laugh. Em put her hands to her head.

"Oh wait, I'm getting something else." She said.

"What? What is it?" Devon said, fighting a mild panic.

"I think I know how our night is going to end," Em said with a wide smile.

"Oh, and how's that?" Devon asked, arching an eyebrow.

Em slid her hands around Devon's waist, resting her hands comfortably inside her front pockets.

"I see us eating one plate of s'mores then going back to my place."

"Hmm, and what's going to happen once we get there?" Devon asked, playfully bumping into Em.

"Well, that's interesting."

"Tell me more," Devon said.

"I see us having the best sex either of us has ever had." Devon felt her core tighten. A heat rose up her body, settling low in her stomach.

"We could skip the s'mores." Devon suggested.

"Nope, sorry. The s'mores were part of the vision. Besides, who skips s'mores?" Devon gave a tiny whimper as Em pulled her in tight against her body.

"Okay, then. I suggest we go ahead and get these s'mores then," Devon said, trapping her lower lip between her teeth.

Devon had never felt the need to rush through eating a s'more before. Emilia seemed to be taking her time, savoring every bite. The ease with which the woman paced herself was enough to push Devon over the edge of desire. Who was this woman that had her so in a frenzy?

"Ready to go?" Em asked, her tone had taken on a bit of a rasp. A signal that Em was done toying with her.

"Oh, I don't know. Why rush? Maybe we could get our faces painted while we're here." Devon grinned, studying Em's face. Check one for her.

"We could stay, if that's what you want. Or we could go make our own fun," Em said, her voice a hushed whisper. She moved a strand of Devon's red hair out of the way and kissed her neck. The sensation made Devon smile and gave her goosebumps up and down her arms.

"Now that I think of it, I think I like that idea better," Devon said, her own voice becoming a whisper.

"Should we tell Jamie bye?"

"I'll text him once we're on the way." The last thing Devon wanted was for her brother to get in the middle of her first night with Em.

The drive to Em's home was torture. She had been right to text Jamie after they left. He had tried to get her to stay for one more s'more. An idea that she would have undoubtedly relented to had they been face to face. She had always had a hard time telling her baby brother no.

Em's home looked large in the street lights. It struck Devon that if she didn't know Em the house might be a bit foreboding. Now, as she pulled into the driveway there was nowhere else she'd rather be. A night with just her and Em - the thought teased at the corners of her brain.

At the door she gave a courtesy knock and waited for Em's voice before she entered. Em had already started a fire in the large stone fireplace. The flames lit the room in a warm cozy glow. Devon walked to the couch and sat, admiring the room around her.

"I meant to tell you earlier, I like your scarf," Em said, a smile playing across her lips.

"You do?" Devon asked. Em sat beside her on the couch. She grabbed the ends of the scarf, gently pulling Devon closer.

"I do. I think it must be important to you." The words surprised Devon, there was no way Em could have known where the scarf came from.

"Thanks. My grandmother made it for me." Em gave a simple nod of her head. She unwound the scarf from around her neck, then carried the scarf to a peg on the wall.

"Now we'll know it's safe," Em said, her same warm smile never wavered. Devon was taken aback by Em's sweetness.

"Thanks, it's pretty old at this point."

"Then a little extra care is just what it needs." Devon found herself smiling at Em, her head cocked to one side.

"What? Why are you looking at me that way?" Em asked with a chuckle.

"You're too sweet for your own good," Devon said. She wrapped her arms around Em's waist and pulled until they were both lying on the couch. Em smiled above her, leaning down to kiss Devon across the lips. The throb returned to the place between Devon's thighs. Em seemed to sense her tension. She let her hand slide inside Devon's pants. Her fingers teasing the wet spot forming on Devon's underwear. Devon gave a whimper as Em's fingers tucked inside her underwear. There was too much between them. Devon undid her jeans and lifted her hips. Em helped pull her jeans off. She paused, taking a moment to appreciate Devon's black lace underwear before pulling them down as well. Devon sat up pulling her sweater and bra off in one single movement. She thought she saw Em bite her lower lip. *Good,* Devon thought. It was about time for Em to be as off kilter as she felt.

She watched as Em took off her own shirt and pants. Em bent low to continue kissing her and Devon unclasped her bra. She marveled at Em's beauty in the firelight. Her skin, pale and warm in the glow. Devon's hands wanted to travel the pathways across Em's body. Wanted to explore all her roads. She slid her hands across the smooth skin of Em's back, cupping her hands against her ass. Em's kisses grew deeper and more passionate.

Em kissed her way from Devon's earlobe down to her left breast. Her lips fastened against her nipple and gave a powerful suck. Devon arched her back, digging her fingers into Em's shoulder. Em continued her trail of kisses past Devon's ribs, her navel, finally arriving at her core. Devon sucked in a breath as Em slid her tongue inside her. Her arms found the nearest couch cushion, she dug her nails into it. Em's tongue slid across Devon's clit making slow circles. A moan caught in Devon's throat, her orgasm taking even her by surprise.

Chapter 8

Em lay her head against Devon's chest. The world seemed to fracture. The version of her from high school still in a state of shock by what had just happened. Perfect Devon, the girl who had teased her teenage fantasies was lying underneath her. On her couch. Naked and better than any dream she'd ever had. The current version of herself looked at Devon with much clearer eyes. Devon was beautiful, and smart, and funny, and sexy. But like everyone she had her own flaws. Em thought Devon was all the more beautiful because of her idiosyncrasies no matter how slight. Devon twirled a strand of her dark hair between her fingers.

"It's still wild being here with you after all this time."

"What do you mean? You didn't think we'd end up naked on my couch when we first met?"

"You were like thirteen when I met you, so no."

"Ahh, that's right and you were a mature fifteen back then. Far too old for me," Em teased. Devon gave her a playful poke to the side and Em squirmed.

"I don't know, you were Jamie's friend. I never really saw past that."

"And how about now?"

"Now I think Jamie and I are going to be fighting over you." Devon chuckled.

"Okay, but you should know your brother fights dirty."

"Oh, I'm aware."

Em let a long moment of silence hang between them. She enjoyed the rise and fall of Devon's chest. The scent of Devon's shampoo, lemon and peppermint surrounded Em. She was afraid to speak, to lose the moment. Afraid of watching what they had created together unravel before her eyes. It was Devon who broke the silence first.

"I have a dinner with a few friends from the University tomorrow night. It's nothing fancy. But most of them have a plus one to bring. Would you like to come?"

"Hmmm, are you saying I'm your plus one?"

"I would like for you to be if you want. No pressure, if it's too soon for you I understand. I just thought..." Devon's words spilled out in a jumble until Em put a finger up to her lips.

"Shhh. If you want me there, then I want to come." Em lifted her head, brushing a soft kiss against Devon's lips.

"I want you there," Devon said simply. It was enough for Em, to know that she was wanted.

"Do you want to spend the night?" Em asked. She checked the fireplace; the last bit of the fire was dying out. The cold would creep in soon, the way it did in most older homes.

"Are you asking me to have a sleepover?"

"Mmmhmm, I was thinking we could watch makeup tutorials and do each other's hair," Em said teasing.

"Oh, then I'm in. Have you ever watched those hair dye fails videos? Tragic." Devon teased. Em shook her head, but forced herself to stand. Her body immediately missed Devon's warmth.

"Well, come on then, my bedroom TV awaits." Devon took her hand and followed her upstairs. Em slid the covers of her bed back, allowing Devon to crawl under the warm covers first. Once she was situated, Em climbed inside. She smiled as Devon scooted her body as close to hers as possible.

"Are you cold?" Em asked, silently cursing herself for not turning her heat up.

"Not anymore," Devon said into her ear. The sensation of the whisper against her ear lobe sent shivers through Em's body. Devon slid a hand down Em's body, settling it between her thighs.

"I knew I was going to enjoy sleeping over with you," Em said, her voice cracking with want.

"Seriously, in like a psychic way?" Devon said, suddenly serious. Em gave a laugh.

"No, not in a psychic way. Trust me, it doesn't take a psychic to guess that spending the night with you is going to be fun," Em teased. Devon chuckled. Her fingers gently stroked against Em's clit. She rested her head against Devon's shoulder as pleasure built between her thighs. When her orgasm hit a loud sigh escaped her. Em felt Devon's arms encircle her, pulling her body close. There was no rush. The night was young and it felt as though they had all the time in the world to explore one another. Em pushed Devon's red hair behind her shoulder and gave her a kiss on the neck.

"I told you this was going to be fun." Em smirked.

"I'm just getting started with you." Devon smiled back. Em felt heat rising inside her again. She gave Devon's neck another kiss.

Em reached for the remote and as promised turned on a failed hair video. A girl came on showing how she planned to bleach her hair. The video ended with her hair a bright yellowy white color. Em settled into the moment, watching Devon's chest rise and fall beside her. Sleep came all too quickly to claim them both.

In the morning, Em woke and found her bed empty. A stinging disappointment filled her chest. She hadn't expected Devon to ditch her without saying goodbye. *The perils of modern dating,* Em said. *Devon had early classes this morning,* she reminded herself. *Maybe she had to leave and didn't want to disturb me.* Em liked that line of thinking far better, and it fit Devon's personality.

She walked downstairs and was startled to find Devon sitting at her kitchen counter. Devon wore a pair of black headphones as she cooked eggs at the stove. The sight of it warmed Em's heart. She was careful not to scare Devon, walking around to her side and giving a wave to get her attention. A huge smile broke across Devon's face when she saw Em. She removed the headphones.

"Good morning."

"Good morning, sorry I didn't hear you get up."

"That's alright, I kept you pretty busy last night." Devon smirked. Flashes from the night before flew through Em's mind. Devon waking her up at 3 a.m. for some extra attention. They hadn't gotten back to sleep until well after 6 a.m... Em cocked an eyebrow.

"Speaking of which, how are you awake right now?"

"I'm used to waking up for early morning classes." Devon shrugged. Then looking at her watch she gave a frown.

"Speaking of early classes, I have time for a bite of breakfast and then I have to get going." Devon made two plates of eggs and handed one to Em.

"I understand." I'm glad I woke up so that I could tell you bye.

"Don't be silly, I would have woken you up long enough to tell you goodbye," Devon said with a casual chuckle. There was something in the forthrightness of her response that pulled Em in further. She wouldn't have *just left without saying goodbye,* Em thought to herself. Devon might as well be the moon, and Em was the tide pulled in or pushed out by her gravity.

They ate their eggs and chatted excitedly about the day ahead. The morning felt so natural, as if they had played this scene together a thousand times.

"I'm so glad you're coming to dinner with me tonight. It's hard being the only one there without someone to bring."

"Well, I'm always happy to be your arm candy."

"Mmm well, you will make me look good that's for sure."

"What's the dress code?"

"No dress code. Most people go business casual. So anything along those lines will be fine. We're meeting at Fox and Otter 7:00."

"I'll be there." Em said.

"Perfect. I really do have to get going. Thanks again for reintroducing me to S'mores Fest."

"Of course, I had a blast." Devon gave her a small kiss on the cheek. Grabbed her red scarf from the peg on the wall. Then she was gone.

Em sat back in her chair at the kitchen table. Her home had a sudden feeling of lack. It caught her off guard. In all her mornings before she had been perfectly content to sit and eat breakfast by herself. Now, though, she found herself with a sense of longing. Of missing something that was supposed to be there but wasn't. Em shook her head and stood. She loaded her plate in the dishwasher and went about her normal morning routine. Until she checked her phone.

Shit, she said aloud to herself. There were well over ten missed messages from Jamie. She really needed to find her best friend a boyfriend or convince him to adopt a dog. Every message was basically the same. He wanted to know exactly what happened between her and Devon. Em rolled her eyes and grinned to herself. She decided to skip all formality. Jamie answered her call on the second ring.

"Where have you been? I've been texting all morning."

"I know, I can see that. I was a bit preoccupied."

"Ha! I knew it. You and my sister were together," Jamie said as though he had discovered the solution to some great mystery.

"Of course I was with her," Em said with a grin.

"Did you want all the details?" Em asked.

"Oh, no. Thank you. That won't be necessary," Jamie said. Em could imagine the look on his face. A grin spread wide across her own face.

"But… I do want to know how it went?" Jamie said.

"The night went very well." Em said.

"Very well, like she's moving into your place? Or very well, like it was just a good time?"

"Neither." Em said simply.

"EMMMmmm," Jamie whined.

"What?"

"You have to give me more than this."

"It was one night, Jamie. Hardly enough to ask her to move in. But it was a good time and I would like to explore our connection further."

"Thank you, for keeping things so poetic. At least where Devon is concerned."

"What can I say, Devon brings out my more poetic nature."

"Are you falling for her?" Jamie asked. The question struck Em, and she did not know the answer. Her silence was too long for Jamie's liking.

"It's okay to not know the answer. Sometimes it takes time to grapple with feelings." The truth of the statement struck her. If there was anyone in her life who understood the complicated relationship one has with their emotions, it was Jamie. They had met as teens, right after his family had moved to Nightshade. Jamie had always been different. He had never quite fit in anywhere. Nightshade was a new start. But almost as soon as his family arrived, he had found himself in the grips of a major depression. Em remembered those early days, seeing him in the lunchroom always by himself. So one day she had decided to sit with him. It had taken him a whole week to even speak a word to her, but slowly he had warmed. She had introduced him to her tight circle of friends and invited him to join the drama club. It was there that Jamie had found a place to belong. And in wearing many faces, he found the little bits he needed for himself. Those days were past him, but there were times he still struggled. Having a friend like Em didn't keep him from struggling. But having someone who was there for him when those moments hit meant everything in the world to him.

"Thank you, Jamie."

"Of course. And for what it's worth I think the two of you looked really good together. Not just physically, I mean you truly work together." Internally, Em's heart exploded with warmth.

"I think so too." Em said silently into the phone. They were quiet for a few moments until Em broke it once again.

"I'm having dinner with Devon's work friends tonight. Do you have any advice?"

"Do you remember Devon's friend Jessica?"

"From high school?"

"That's the one. She's working at the university. I would steer clear of her. She can be a bit petty, and there's nothing she likes more than showing Devon up."

"I'll keep that in mind." Em said. This night just got a bit more interesting. In high school Jessica had always been number two, just one step away from Devon who was number one. Apparently, the dynamic had followed them into adulthood.

"I can't wait to hear the details tomorrow," Jamie said. Em could hear the cackle in his tone.

"Yeah, nothing better than high school drama as an adult." They both laughed. Times like this, Em realized how much she appreciated this strange friendship they had carved out with each other.

Chapter 9

Devon examined herself in the mirror for the thousandth time. Tonight, Em would be meeting her friends from the college. Her nerves had set in almost immediately after she left Em's house. Devon had a good feeling about Em fitting in with her friends, with one exception. Jessica Stewart. She and Jessica had been doing this dance for as long as Devon could remember. The only person in her list of contacts that she was sorta, kinda, but not really friends with. If she had one concern it was that Jessica would be spending the night comparing Em to her newest shiniest boyfriend. The sad thing was Devon actually liked Jessica's boyfriend, Jake.

Devon looked at herself in the mirror. She wore a long-sleeved white shirt with gray stripes, the shirt was a Fall favorite for her. She partnered the shirt with a navy blue cardigan and her gray work pants. Devon appraised her appearance once again, she looked good.

"I am comfortable with who I am. I can handle any social situation." Devon recited to her reflection in the mirror. A knock on her door broke the spell. *Shit.* That meant Em was here and the night was officially beginning. She opened the doors and stood awestruck.

Em's outfit was simple, but that didn't diminish how amazing she looked in any way. She wore a white sweater with jeans, and a green denim jacket. All her clothes hung well on her body, hugging her in an attractive way.

"Wow, you look amazing." Devon said.

"You don't look half bad yourself." Em leaned forward giving Devon a kiss on the cheek.

"I should probably give you fair warning before we get there about…"

"Jessica Stewart?" Em sent Devon a wink.

"Actually yes. Oh my gosh, was that a psychic thing?" Devon asked, her eyebrows shooting up. Em burst into laughter.

"No, that was from Jamie. He warned me this morning."

"Oh yeah, what did he say?"

"Are you sure you want to know? I mean this is your friend we're talking about."

"Tell me. I wouldn't exactly call us friends."

"Fair enough. He said she was petty, and that she enjoys one-upping you."

"That's a pretty accurate assessment."

"If you don't mind me asking. Why put yourself in the same place with a person who treats you that way?"

"That's a fair question. I guess it comes down to her being my oldest relationship in town outside of Jamie. You know, like I've known her so long that at this point it would be weird if we weren't in each other's lives."

"I guess," Em said, her confusion evident.

"Don't you have anyone like that in your life?"

"Not really," Em admitted, chewing on her lower lip as she searched for her thoughts.

"Life is too short for bad sushi or bad friendships." Devon nodded.

"That's pretty great life advice," Devon said with a chuckle.

"Stick around. I'm brimming with wisdom." Em smirked. Devon had the sudden desire to kiss Em. She wanted to kiss her until that smirk became a plea. The same way she had last night. Hopefully, those things would come later.

The Fox and Otter was a playfully stoic bar in town. An establishment that poked fun at itself by teasing the fact that it took things too seriously. They had a long list of rules, 50 in fact, listed on a sign out front. Such as rule number 29 which was not wearing a brown belt on Fridays and Saturdays. Rule number fifty was to disregard rules 1-49. Devon and her friends hung out once a month consistently. Jessica had picked The Fox and Otter because of its centralized location. The bar was located at the very middle point of town, a coincidence too good not to take advantage of.

Devon's friends had secured their normal table. Located in the very back of the dining area, their table was long enough to fit twelve people and had the surrounding area to itself. Devon took a breath as she walked in. Her hand reached out for Em's as if acting of its own volition. Em met her eyes with a warm smile. Em had the most beautiful eyes Devon had ever seen, a deep bright green. She could spend time getting lost in those eyes, trying to figure out the thoughts behind them.

At the table, all the regulars were assembled. Jessica and Jake sat towards the head of the table, of course. Jake wore a mustard-colored sweater that matched the top Jessica wore.

Devon could have laughed at the scene, but to do so would be rude. Beside them sat Levi and his partner Oliver. Levi worked in the Psychology Department with Devon, while Oliver worked in the business and recruitment office with Jessica. At the other end of the table sat Quinn, the seat beside her noticeably empty. Quinn was in charge of recruitment, beautiful on the inside and the outside.

"Hey guys." Devon said as they approached. She saw Jessica's eyes land on Em, and the slight twitch of her eyebrow.

"Devon, hello. We've been waiting for you. We didn't realize you had a plus one. Jake, be a sweetie and bring Devon and her friend an extra chair." Jake dutifully brought over an extra chair, a large smile across his face. Devon appreciated Jake's easy manner and frequent smiles. He was intelligent, one of the prize professors of the Math department. Unlike many of his colleagues, Jake found relating to his students easy. This had made him one of the most popular instructors on campus.

"Hi, Devon, who's your friend?" Jake asked, placing the chair in an empty spot beside Quinn. Devon sat and Em quickly followed suit. She could tell from Em's expression that she was still taking the situation in.

"Everyone, this is Em. And Em, this is Quinn, Oliver, Levi,

Jake and you probably remember Jessica from high school." Her friends all gave their polite greetings. Em smiled warmly and gave a polite wave.

At the end of the table Jessica studied Em. Devon had made the executive decision to get what was bound to be a semi-awkward situation out of the way up front.

"Em, I'm so sorry. But I can't seem to place you from high school."

"Emilia Thorne. We didn't exactly run in the same circles. I was in the drama club, Jamie is one of my best friends."

"Emilia Thorne, seriously? Oh, that can't be you."

"In the flesh."

"You look amazing. I didn't recognize you at all."

"Thanks," Em responded politely.

"Not that you didn't look nice in high school. I just. Well, I only mean that you really grew into yourself." Jessica amended with a smile. Devon had to admit that Jessica's response was better than she'd expected. Jessica was being cordial, bordering on kind.

"Thank you, that's sweet of you to say. I'm definitely more

comfortable in my own skin these days," Em said, she smiled at Jessica and Devon knew it was genuine.

"Em, I haven't seen you around campus. Do you work at the University?" Jake asked, he stretched his arm around the back of Jessica's chair. Devon felt a fondness for Jake, she hoped that Jessica realized what a find she had in the man.

"I don't. I attended years ago and studied the sciences. I enjoyed my time there, but my path lay elsewhere." Em said with a shrug and a smile. Quinn had been sitting in relative silence. The woman was usually one of the more lively in the group. Quinn had auburn hair which was usually tied up; tonight, it fell loose down her back. Her sweatshirt was cute, but far from her normal attire. Devon deduced that perhaps Quinn and her longtime girlfriend Jackie may be going through one of their *off* phases. Quinn looked at Em and seemed to be studying her face. After a long moment a smile replaced her solemn expression.

"Oh hey, I know you." Quinn said to Em.

"Have we met before?" Em asked.

"I don't know you know you. But you're the Nightshade Apothecary, aren't you?" A spark lit in Em's eyes.

"The Nightshade Apothecary?" Jessica asked, confusion

clearly written across her face. Devon herself turned to study Em's reaction.

"Oh, that was ages ago," Em laughed.

"You were amazing!"

"Can you explain to me what the Nightshade Apothecary is?" Jessica asked, clearly growing flustered.

"Oh, Jessica, she had a podcast and a vlog. She talked about psychic and natural remedies. I found the information you gave really helpful. I still use one of the tinctures you suggested on the podcast," Quinn said.

"I'm so glad you enjoyed it," Em said. Devon's head felt like it might explode.

"How did I not know this?" Devon asked, her tone more abrupt than she had meant for it to be.

"You never asked." Em smirked.

"Why did you stop? If you don't mind me asking," Quinn asked. Devon watched as everyone turned, giving Em their full attention.

"It was a hard decision, but I stepped away to focus on a new project. I own a store in town now called Natural Wonders."

"Oh, I love that place. You have some great rocks, crystals, and minerals," Jake said.

"Thank you, I try to get the best of what I stock."

"It shows. I have several items I've bought from your store on display in my office."

"I'm honored," Em said. It was obvious she took great pride in her store.

"So wait a minute... You had a successful podcast on natural remedies and psychics? Here in Nightshade? Are you a psychic?" Jessica's questions came out as rapid fire. Em quickly glanced at Devon, as if asking for permission to be honest. Devon sent her a warm smile and subtle nod in response.

"Yes, I had a podcast on natural remedies and psychics. And yes, I did it here in Nightshade. Also yes, I am a psychic, but I don't give readings much anymore." Jessica sat back in her chair, obviously sorting out the information she'd been given.

The dinner progressed pretty normally after that. Quinn finally revealed that she had in fact broken up with Jackie. Everyone tried their best to be supportive, though this was break-up number five between the two women.

"Don't think for a minute I'm not going to press you for answers about this later," Devon said with a grin.

"I don't have any secrets from you. You just have to ask the right questions," Em said, a smirk hanging from her lips.

"I can't wait to get you home." The words came out before Devon could hold them back. Em's eyebrow shot up once more.

"Oh yeah, you in a rush to get back home?" Em smirked.

"I don't want to share you any longer than I have to," Devon returned. She watched as Em worried her lower lip with her teeth. Em could be frustratingly difficult to read, but if she had a tell this was it. Devon had picked up on it last night when they were together.

"Does that turn you on?" Devon whispered into Em's ear. Around them, her friends were laughing at a story Jake had just told. Em turned her face into Devon's ear.

"Mmmhmm, it does. But why don't you keep me invested. It's going to be a long night after all." Devon bit back a whimper, Em smirked. She had flipped the tables on her. Devon was more turned on by Em's tease than she'd like to admit to herself. She turned and locked eyes with Em. The same fire now raging inside her, burned inside of Em as well. Devon could see it reflected back to her in the emerald green of Em's eyes. She reached over, laying a hand on Em's thigh, drawing slow circles.

"I don't understand why the University decided to cut the budget for the Fall Festival this year. It's the school's largest fundraiser. How am I supposed to get vendors at this budget?" Jessica groaned. Devon continued her circles, refusing to spare a glance in Em's direction.

"What sort of vendors are you looking for?" The question from Em jolted Devon. Jessica also glanced at Em, surprise registered on her face.

"Well, we have all the slots for food vendors filled. But we could really use some fun vendors. People selling crafts, or soaps. Hell, I would hire someone to paint faces at this point," Jessica said, flustered.

"Any interest in having a psychic?" Em asked simply. It drove Devon wild, the smoothness of Em's tone. Devon notched her hand higher up Em's thigh. She thought she saw Em swallow.

"A psychic? You mean, you want to be a vendor?" Jessica asked.

"Sure, if it helps out. I could do a set up for Natural Wonders and then also offer psychic readings." Em shrugged, but Devon could see the strain on her face. She gave Em's thigh a squeeze.

"Yes, that would be amazing! That's just the sort of thing I was looking for."

"Well, then it's settled."

"Thank you so much for being willing to help out," Jessica said. Her tone told Devon that she was truly grateful. Em sat back in her seat. The rest of Devon's friends went back to their conversations. Em covered Devon's hand with her own, moving it up even farther on her thigh. She squeezed Devon's hand tighter around her thigh. Devon felt her breath catch, almost choking on the air in her own lungs. Em leaned in painfully close, her lips a tickle against her ear.

"Are you ready to leave?" Em asked. Devon couldn't stand the anticipation any longer.

"I think we're going to head out. I have an early day tomorrow," Devon said to her friends. They turned, studying her, perhaps closer than she was comfortable with.

"We haven't even ordered food yet," Jessica mused, a wide smile across her face. *Shit.* She could probably read the subtext written all over Devon's face.

"Which makes the timing perfect," Em interrupted, standing and pulling Devon up with her. The others chuckled as they walked out to the parking lot.

"I think that went well." Devon giggled. She was surprised when Em pressed her hands against her hips, moving her backwards. Em didn't stop until Devon's back rested against her car. She leaned in, kissing Devon hard on the mouth.

"Sorry, I've just been waiting to do that tonight." Em said, wiping her lips with one finger. Between her thighs, Devon felt herself grow wet. The pulsing throb low at her core deepened. Devon fumbled with her keys, finally managing to unlock the door of her car. She and Em both loaded hastily.

As she pulled from the parking lot Devon felt Em slide her hand on top of her thigh. She guessed turnabout really was fair play in this case. Devon kept her eyes on the road as her body screamed to pay attention to Em. There was no way to know exactly what would happen once they stepped through the door of her home. But one thing was certain, Devon's desire for Em was a wild, untamable thing. Never in her days had her body been so undone by a woman. All Devon could hope was that Em would put her back together again once she had squeezed every ounce of pleasure from her body.

Chapter 10

Devon pulled into her parking spot so quickly that her car jolted to a stop. Em smiled to herself, knowing she was to blame for Devon's haste. Devon's desire wasn't one-sided. Em had barely been able to keep it together at the restaurant. Her thigh was still warm from Devon's touch.

Em watched smiling as Devon fretted with her keys. Unable to resist the urge to tease, Em slid her hands around Devon's waist from behind. Em felt Devon suck a tight breath in. She had Devon right where she wanted her. Em slid her hands inside the front pockets of Devon's pants. Devon groaned, her head coming forward to lean against the door with a slight thud.

"You gotta give me a break. I'm never going to get this door opened," Devon teased.

"Here, let me help you with that," Em said as she grabbed Devon's hand, guiding the key inside the lock. Devon gave the knob a turn and they almost fell inside as the door opened.

Em's hands found Devon's waist this time pushing her

against the wall, she kicked the door closed with her foot. Their lips locked together, Em had been wanting this all night. No, not just wanting. Needing. She had needed the uninterrupted feel of Devon's lips against her own. Now that they were here Em was reluctant to tear their lips apart, instead she reached down undoing her pants first, then Devon's. She slid Devon's pants down and watched as the woman kicked them away. Em was grateful when Devon helped her push her own jeans down.

She finally took a moment, forcefully pulling back her mouth. Em took in the sight of Devon, standing there, wearing her navy cardigan and a black thong. She fought the urge to take Devon down to the ground right there in the entryway. Instead, she allowed Devon to take her hand and lead her into the living room. Their lips came together naturally, as if they missed being together. Em hooked her fingers inside Devon's thong sliding it down Devon's body. In a heartbeat they were undressing one another, the remainder of their clothing in a pile on the living room floor.

Em knelt in front of Devon. Em's hands parted Devon's thighs. Her tongue quickly found Devon's clit, teasing it. Devon's hips bucked, causing her to bump hard against Em's face. Em slipped her hands between Devon's thighs widening them further. Her hands traced the way up Devon's butt grabbing

her hips. Em spread Devon's thighs wider with her elbows and pulled her down until she was squatting against her mouth. As she held the contact between them, she struggled to pull Devon closer against her mouth. It wasn't enough to be close, Em wanted her and Devon to be practically connected. Em lay back on the carpet, pulling at Devon bringing her down with her . She helped ease Devon into position until her core was lined up with Em's mouth. Em's fingers pulled Devon's folds apart gently. Devon gasped as Em pressed her tongue lightly against her clit. She flicked gently, her tongue a soft tease.

As her tongue gained momentum, so did Devon's hips. She thrust against Em's face in time. Em could feel Devon's pleasure building, spurring her to go faster. To go harder. Until Devon's body collapsed on top of her, pleasure overtaking her. Em continued to slowly rub her tongue against Devon's clit, helping her ride out the aftershocks. Devon eased her body down to the place beside Em on the carpet.

"That was…"

"Well, pretty mind-blowing if I'm honest." Devon said.

"I think you're always pretty mind-blowing," Em said with a slight smile.

"I didn't hurt your neck did I?"

"No, not at all," Em said. She curled in beside Devon, kissing her ear. Devon leaned into the kiss.

"You know what I think?" Devon whispered into Em's ear.

"Tell me," Em said. Her voice cracked and she didn't care.

"I think it's your turn next," Devon said. She pushed Em onto her back. Her hands trailed down Em's body leaving the ghost of her touch behind her fingertips. She spread Em's folds, opening her up. Devon stuck her tongue inside her, pressing as far as possible. She thrust in and out several times, delighted when Em had to grab at the carpet to steady herself. Devon moved her tongue in circles causing Em to buck wildly. She pressed an arm against Em's belly holding her firmly in place, pulling a groan from her. Devon's tongue slid out finding its way to Em's clit. Em gasped, her hands reaching out. Em's fingers tangled in Devon's hair as she pulled the woman closer. Her orgasm was a fireworks show inside her body, she saw a kaleidoscope of colors and felt her very bones quake with the intensity.

Devon rolled to the side and Em felt a trickle of sweat roll down her brow.

"That was... amazing."

"Thanks, what can I say? You bring out the best in me." They migrated to the kitchen for snacks. Devon grabbed her old charcuterie board and loaded it with crackers, meats, and cheeses. Then took Em to her bedroom for cuddles. Devon turned on the TV and they watched while they lay in bed eating.

"So all that stuff at dinner, I had no idea," Devon said with a lazy smile.

"I wasn't trying to hide it from you," Em said, a little caught off guard by the defensiveness in her own voice.

"I know. Especially if it was a long time ago. I understand it just not coming up. I guess I just want to hear more about it. Unless it's a sensitive subject." Em cursed herself for having made Devon feel like any topic was off limits. It was a poke to an old bruise, but nothing she was incapable of speaking about. She turned to face Devon.

"That was a really good time in my life. But it was also a pretty awful time because I lost a friendship that meant a lot to me."

"Oh no, babe, I'm sorry. You don't have to talk about it if you don't want to."

"No, it's okay. It'll probably fill in some gaps for you."

"When I was in college I met Helen. She and I were thrown into a room together but we became best friends very quickly. We spent all our time together; I think we actually made your brother a bit jealous."

"Not that he would ever admit to that."

"Of course not."

"So were the two of you... like together?"

"No, just friends. Helen was straight. That's where our trouble started."

"How so?"

"After college, she met a guy and they started dating. Helen knew I was a psychic; I was pretty open about it in those days. I had my podcast and vlog. So, she started asking me for advice about this guy. What could I pick up about him? At first, she was grateful for my insights. But as time went on, I just sensed that there was something going on with this guy that wasn't good. I told her as much. She told me that I was making things up for attention. We didn't speak much after that. They got engaged and she cut me out of her life."

"I'm so sorry babe. That's awful."

"It felt like mourning a death. But she was still alive, and that made it worse."

"Is that when you decided to pull away from..." Devon's words trailed off as she searched for the right thing to say.

"When you decided to pull away from that part of your life?"

"It is what pushed me to finally make the decision. But the truth is I had plenty of people in my life who helped me make that decision. Psychics have a bad rap for giving good news all the time, we're called fakes. But no one loves the bearer of bad news. People are upset either way."

"I think I understand what you're saying. If you're up for hearing it, I did notice something at dinner."

"Of course, I always want to hear your thoughts."

"It sounded like you miss that being part of your day to day life. And I was a little surprised when you signed up for the Fall Festival."

"I do miss it. I'm looking for a way to incorporate it into my life, without it becoming my entire life. I suppose the Fall Festival is an easy way to do that because I can make it fun.

There's less pressure when it's not meant to be serious."

"Well, I'm proud of you for taking a step towards bringing that side of yourself out again. I'm sorry you've had so many experiences of people in your life not responding well to that part of you."

"Thanks, yeah it can be rough. It's taught me to be careful about who I let into my life. Some people are really freaked out by me being a psychic. Others see me as some strange novelty and use me to get attention.

"Have you met my friend Em? She's a psychic. Isn't that fun and quirky?" Em said, in a fakely sweet tone.

"Oh god, that does sound awful. I hope it didn't feel that way tonight with my friends."

"Not at all. Tonight was a lot of fun. I felt very safe being my authentic self. And after the restaurant wasn't so bad either." Em took Devon's hand giving her a sweeping kiss along her knuckle.

"I'm glad you felt so comfortable. And I'm glad you told me about how people have approached relationships with you in the past."

"Thank you for going out of your way to make me

comfortable."

The two lay in stillness with the TV playing in the background. Devon twirled Em's hair absentmindedly between her fingers. Em could feel sleep tugging at her, she rolled her body closer to Devon's. Sleep came, and Em didn't resist.

Chapter 11

Devon hurried through her house. She was running late, per usual. These days with Em had been enthralling. But Em also had a way of providing the most delightful distractions.

"Em, have you seen my star earrings?"

"You left them in the bathroom," Em called.

"Thanks, babe."

"Tell me again why college students are getting a field trip with chaperones?" Em called.

"Because they're basically oversized pre-schoolers. But we don't call ourselves chaperones," Devon said, coming back to the living room with earrings in hand. She started to poke one through. Em slid in behind her kissing her neck. It raised the hair on the back of her neck up, and sent a jolt through her system. Devon paused, momentarily relenting to the kiss.

"What do you call yourselves?" Em purred, her breath tickling her ear.

"Coordinators." Devon gave a laugh. She knew the answer was ridiculous. From behind her, she heard Em give a chuckle against the skin of her neck. Last night had been amazing. Em had met her friends, and she had seemed to fit in a way that Devon hadn't expected. Her friends had been mostly curious about Em being a psychic. The secret flirting at dinner had been electrifying. The sex when they made it back to her place had been some of the best in her life. But what had stuck out to Devon most was that Em had allowed her in. Em had her walls, just as most people did. Last night, Em had opened her gates and let Devon come inside. Devon felt connected to her in a way she hadn't before. The sort of connection that can only come when you know a person's past hurts and see them for who they truly are.

"Whatever you call yourselves I'm glad you invited me to come along. I'm remiss to say that I've never been to an apple orchard before."

"What? How is that even possible? Hawk Mountain Orchard is like five minutes from your home."

"I guess I never had a reason to go before."

"What do you mean?"

"I'm sorry it never occurred to me to just go commune with the apple trees before." They both broke into laughter.

"Well then, I'm glad I can be your apple orchard first." Em gave Devon's neck a playful nip before kissing her again. Devon could sink deep into those kisses. She wanted to let Em take her away to another place. A new place where it was just the two of them. But she reminded herself that no such place existed. She forced herself to put in her final earring.

"Thanks for letting me borrow some clothes," Em shrugged, looking down at her outfit. Devon turned and took in the sight of her for the first time that morning. Em wore one of her oversized sweatshirts, brandishing the Nightshade University logo. A pair of her jeans that Devon had been sure wouldn't fit Em, somehow looked better on her.

"Anytime, I happen to like the way you wear them."

"Do you now?"

"Mmmhmm, I do. Of course, I like you better without any clothes on at all," Devon said, allowing a moment of boldness to overtake her. She grabbed Em by the hips, pulling her close. Em let out a tiny gasp and it spurred Devon to give her the slightest kiss on the lips.

"You ready to head out? We have adult humans to corral." Em giggled.

"Well, we wouldn't want the adult humans to wander about without their coordinators."

"Exactly. That would be just asking for a disaster." They grinned at each other. Devon followed Em out. The day was gorgeous, and she was more than a little excited to be going to the orchard with Em.

Hawk Mountain Orchard was one of Devon's favorite places in Nightshade. Rows of apple trees lined the huge orchard and a small gravel drive welcomed visitors to drive through. Devon was reminded how much she enjoyed being out of town. She loved Nightshade, but there was something magical about getting into nature. The orchard was what Devon would consider a romantic place. Growing up in town she had been on several dates here through the years. Blankets set up under a tree to watch the passing night sky, or picnics on the hill overlooking the tree rows. Today she had brought everything needed to have those kinds of experiences with Em.

"I couldn't help notice you have your luck jar I gave you up on the mantle. That's a great placement for it."

"I can't thank you enough. Since putting them up and carrying one with me, my luck has never been better."

"So no more runs of bad luck?"

"Not so much as a spilled drink," Devon responded.

"I'm glad I could help. But, I'm glad you had a reason to need my help. Otherwise we might never have come into each other's lives."

"I think you might be right about that. I guess if I can be grateful for any part of Brent's curse, it's that I got to meet you. It almost makes the year of torment worth it."

"My goal is to make it more than worth it."

"Well, you're right on target for getting there."

"I like to hear that I'm doing a good job."

"You're doing a very good job. Especially after last night."

"Oh wow, high praise indeed."

"Well deserved."

"You... um... were pretty amazing, too."

Devon felt a hot blush spread across her cheeks. She wasn't

sure why but Em brought out a shyness in her. She checked in with Becky, the head student coordinator then took Em up the hill overlooking the orchard. She laid a red checked blanket down and gestured for Em to join her. Em glanced out over the horizon and let out a peace filled sigh.

"Do you remember how I told you that in high school I had the biggest crush on you?" Em asked. Devon startled at the directness of the question.

"I remember," Devon said simply.

"I think I must have imagined what it would be like to be with you so many times. What would it be like to go out as your date? What would it be like to take you to bed? I grew out of it, of course. I focused on becoming the person I wanted to be instead of who I wanted to be with. But I have to say based on this past week, this is nothing like what I imagined being with you would be like."

"Oh, I hope that's not a bad thing," Devon said, giving a hard swallow.

"Not at all. It's a wonderful thing. In high school I saw you so one dimensionally. I didn't see past your nice clothes, or pretty hair, or beautiful body. All of which is still true by the way. It's just now I see how earth bendingly beautiful you are as a person. Who you are on the inside is what amazes me now."

"It means a lot to hear you say that. Being popular never felt native to me. My popularity always made me feel like an out of town visitor. When you told me that you'd had a crush on me, do you know what I thought?"

"Tell me."

"Why? I wondered why? You are so interesting. So multifaceted and beautiful. I couldn't imagine why someone as cool as you would ever want to be with someone as boring as me. Even in high school, you were this aloof edgy theater chick, and what was I? The head cheerleader dating the quarterback. It doesn't get much more cliche than that," Devon said with a frown.

"Hey, you are so many things but boring just isn't one of them. I mean for crying out loud, when we met, you were dealing with a hex."

"Oh, I'm sure hexes are a dime a dozen."

"Not really. And as far as high school goes, do you want to know what I remember about you?"

"Sure."

"I remember you being the only girl in school who was popular and nice. I have stories of being made fun of by every other popular kid from high school. But one time I dropped a stack of fliers for the upcoming theater play and you stopped what you were doing and helped me pick them up. Then you asked if I was going to be in the play, and when I said yes you took one of the fliers. I didn't think much of it, except that you were really nice. But then on opening night there you were, sitting close to the stage. That's what I remember you for in high school. Not the head cheerleader. I remember you being this beautiful and kind person," Em said, passion beginning to seep into her tone. She couldn't stand hearing Devon describe herself in any sort of negative light. Devon leaned in, kissing Em hard against the mouth. She pulled away just long enough to whisper into Em's ear.

"Thank you for that. What a beautiful way to be thought of. And I remember that play, you were amazing in it." Devon pulled Em closer, their lips magnetically fixed together.

"Devon, there you are. We've been looking for you." Devon groaned, and Em definitely returned the sentiment. Jessica looked down on them with a flustered expression on her face.

"Were you really just going to stay up here making out?

There's actual work to be done."

"What work?"

"Well, for one, you're here to chaperone."

"Jessica, they're in college. Do they really need hand holding?"

"Well, two of the boys just tried to climb one of the trees. They almost knocked it over so I'm going to say yes," Jessica said sternly. Devon gave a groan, rolling over to her back.

"Honestly, you know freshmen are basically giant toddlers," Jessica scolded.

"Okay, I'm coming." Devon groaned. She rolled over one last time to plant a kiss on Em's lips.

"Keep the blanket warm for me." Devon teased.

"That shouldn't be a problem." Em said, rolling to her back. Devon trudged down the hill. Em was surprised when Jessica sat down beside her on the blanket.

"I'm at my limit for frat boy exploits. Do you mind if I keep you company for two or three minutes?"

"Be my guest." Em chuckled.

"Em, can I ask you a *psychic-like* question?"

"You can ask," Em said, her hesitancy clear.

"What were your thoughts on me and Jake last night?" Jessica asked. Em bit back a groan. She'd been in this position far too many times.

"The two of you look good together," Em offered, knowing this wasn't the answer that Jessica wanted.

"I know we look good, but did it feel right to you?" This time Em sighed out loud.

"How does it feel to you? If you're asking if I got any intuitive hits about your relationship, the answer is no. Jake seems nice and like he enjoys your company. You seemed to enjoy his too."

"I do. I like his company," Jessica interrupted.

"Then what's the problem?" Em asked.

"He's the most stable guy I've ever dated. I hate to admit this, but I'm a little afraid he might wake up one day and go running for the hills."

"I think that you don't know me very well. So you should

probably value your own intuition over mine. What does your heart tell you? Is Jake really the type of guy who goes running for the hills?"

"No, he doesn't. He seems like the kind of guy who would want to work out a problem." Jessica smiled. She bit her lower lip, glancing at Em as if she wanted to say more.

"Why are you looking at me like that?"

"What's up with you and Devon?"

"What do you mean?"

"I mean, the two of you are obviously fond of one another, but what is the thing between you two? What would you call your relationship?" The question caught Em completely off guard.

"I'm not sure there's an answer to that question. We only recently started seeing one another."

"It's just… Well… I don't know… You get what I'm trying to say right?" Em was bewildered. How could someone say so many words and not have made a complete thought?

"No, I have no idea what you're trying to tell me," Em said simply. She wished Jessica would go back to wrangling college kids. A sinking feeling started to form in the back of her brain. She was about to ask Jessica if she shouldn't start heading back down the hill when her thoughts were interrupted.

"It's just the academic and the psychic. It sounds like a wonderful romantic notion. I'm just not sure how it translates to real life." Em knew immediately that this had been the reason Jessica came up the hill in the first place. She did probably have valid questions about Jake, but this seed of doubt was the reason she was here. Jessica stood fluffing her blonde hair out behind her, Em remembered she had the same habit in high school.

"It was good talking to you. It's a beautiful day, don't wait on Devon. No telling when she'll make her way back. You should take advantage of the orchard." Then she was gone. Walking down the hill before Emilia could even form a rebuke. Not that she would have had any idea what to say. She watched the woman go. Em disliked the tiny voice in her head that suggested that Jessica might be right. That perhaps she and Devon didn't fit into each other's worlds. She shook her head, trying to rid herself of the thoughts. Em looked down from the hill, her eyes immediately found Devon. She had put her red hair up in a ponytail and stood talking to two college-age girls. Emilia felt a pang in her heart. As if on cue Devon looked up at her and gave a tiny wave. Inside her chest, Em's heart glowed warm. They were in no rush to define what they were to one another. Em was happy spending time with Devon, she refused to let the likes of Jessica Stewart ruin that for her.

Chapter 12

Devon couldn't put her finger on it, but something was different about Em. Things had started out so well that day, but somewhere along the way there had been a turn. Emilia had drawn in on herself, and no amount of effort on Devon's part seemed to be drawing her out.

In a last ditch effort to save the day Devon had bought snacks and arranged them on the blanket. The gesture had earned her a genuine smile and laugh from Em. Now sitting beside her, Devon couldn't stand the uncomfortable silence.

"Are you mad at me?" Devon asked, her tone tentative. Em's face jerked in her direction.

"Why would I ever be mad at you?"

"I don't know. It's just…well, things were really good. But you've been quiet and reserved. I'm not sure how to take it." Devon blurted out. Em gave a nod of her head.

"I understand. I have a lot on my mind."

"Do you want to talk about it?"

"I'm not sure how to say it."

"Just start slow."

"Earlier when you went to take care of the kids," Em sent her a grin before continuing.

"Jessica stayed behind to talk to me." Devon felt a shudder go through her at the mention of Jessica's name. She listened intently as Em continued.

"Things were fine, she was asking me my psychic impression about Jake. Then she started asking about us. What are we to each other? That kind of thing. She said an academic and a psychic is a romantic story, but she's not sure how it would work out in real life." Devon could have screamed. How dare Jessica butt in where she wasn't wanted or needed?

"I've tried hard not to pay attention to that. But it got me thinking, what are the chances of this being something real?"

"Em, this already is something real. At least for me."

"It is?"

"I know it's early but I don't need more time to be able to

tell you that I already feel deeply for you. It's very different from any previous relationships I've ever had."

"Because I'm a psychic," Em mumbled.

"I hear you grumbling over there," Devon teased.

"And no, it has nothing to do with you being psychic. It's the way you make me feel. The way your eyes light up when you look at me. The way I want to be near you. I've never found that. Not with any other girl." A smile slid across Em's face.

"So you're saying you like me," Em said.

"Yes, I'm saying I like you very much," Devon responded. She was rewarded with a kiss from Em.

"Do me a favor."

"What's that?"

"Next time Jessica opens her big mouth about you and me, please just tell her to fuck right off." Em snorted a laugh. She took a bright crimson-colored apple off the blanket and took a bite.

"You've got it. Next time I see Jessica I'm just going to yell *fuck off* and run away."

"Well, that would certainly get her attention," Devon said

with a chuckle.

"Seriously, I'm sorry she made you feel that way. But if you're ever unsure about something you can always ask me. I can't promise my answer will be what you're hoping to hear but it will always be the truth."

"That's fair. I can make the same promise to you."

"Ooohh, you want to make it a pinky promise?" Devon laughed.

"Sure." Em held out her pinky and Devon looped her own finger around it. They shook on it. Devon watched as the clouds lifted from Em.

"You ready to get out of here?" Devon asked.

"Yep, I'm all yours," Em said leaning in and kissing Devon on the forehead. *I'm all yours*, Devon liked the sound of that.

Their chemistry seemed restored for the drive home, their conversations came naturally. Devon put on the movie *Practical Magic* and settled into her couch with Em. She was glad that things had been so easily resolved. Inside, she still struggled with her anger towards Jessica. *How dare she mess with Em that way? Didn't her own relationship occupy enough of her time?*

The anger stirred inside of her until Devon knew she would have to address it. She grabbed her phone to send *a text message.*

Devon 6 p.m.: *I talked to Em about what you said to her today. It wasn't okay for you to mess with her that way.*

Jessica 6:05 p.m.: *I don't know what you're talking about. I like Emilia, I don't want to see her get hurt.*

Devon 6:05 p.m.: *My relationship with her is none of your business. Besides your words hurt her, not mine.* Devon sent her response quickly, her anger available at her fingertips.

Jessica 6:10 p.m.: *I wasn't trying to hurt her. But I do think it's worth thinking about.*

Devon 6:11 p.m.: *Em and I will handle our relationship.*

The phone went quiet after that. Devon supposed she had made her point, Jessica was most likely pouting. She turned her attention to the more pleasant things around her. Em lay with her head in Devon's lap. Devon played with her hair, letting the strands fall casually between her fingers. Em's dark hair was smooth and soft, with a hint of floral scent from her shampoo.

Devon wasn't sure how it had happened, but somehow

along the way Em had become very important to her. Somehow this was the only place she wanted to be. Right here watching a movie with Em was everything she had always wanted. Time was a strange thing. Devon had spent so much of her adolescence wanting to get as far from Nightshade as possible. Only to have so much of her adulthood pull her right back. Sometimes it was funny how life worked.

"What time is it?" Em asked sleepily.

"It's 8:00. Do you have to get going?"

"I'm afraid so. I need to open the store up early tomorrow. The town opens up its stores for trick or treaters tomorrow."

"And I'm guessing Natural Wonders has something amazing planned."

"You guess correctly. I need to go in tomorrow to set up decorations and get the candy ready."

"Oh, wow, you sound almost giddy," Devon said with a grin.

"That's because I am. This is one of my favorite nights of the Halloween season. I love decorating and getting to see the looks on all the kids' faces. I love walking them around and showing them the rocks and everything else. Kids are so naturally curious, so I get to share the things I love every year."

"Aww, baby, that's so sweet. I didn't realize you were such a softie."

"Only when it comes to kids and animals. No one else gets a pass to my squishy places."

"No one?" Devon asked, a hint of a smile on her lips.

"No one. Except you. You've definitely taken up residence in my squishy parts."

"Aww, babe! If it means anything. You're in my squishy places, too."

"It does. It means everything," Em said her lips grazed Devon's jawline stopping right below her ear.

"So does this mean you'd be okay with me coming by the store tomorrow night? I'd love to see it all set up," Devon said with a grin.

"Umm, yeah. I would be disappointed if you didn't come by," Em said, giving her another kiss, this time across the lips.

"Then tomorrow night it is," Devon said again. She felt a small pang of longing as she watched Em leave. She wished she could snuggle up with the woman. Wished she could fall asleep to the sound of Em's even breathing beside her, and the feel of skin against skin. Instead, Devon finished watching Practical Magic while eating her leftover Chinese food from the night before. A buzz from her phone was a welcome sound. She reached for it hoping that it would be Em, she only felt slight disappointment when it was her brother instead.

"Hey, baby brother. How's life?" Devon said in her sweetest voice.

"Ugh, you know I hate it when you call me baby brother." She could tell Jamie was pouting even over the phone.

"I can't imagine why. After all, you are my baby brother."

"See everyone thinks you're this nice person, but they don't know what I'm forced to endure."

"I know at least one person who likely agrees with you."

"Uh-oh, did you chase someone else over to the dark side? A disgruntled student perhaps?"

"Haha, no, I actually think this might be the founding member of my anti-fan club."

"Oh, do tell."

"It's no one new. Jessica Stewart."

"Oh her."

"You really don't like her, do you?"

"She's always been so nasty to you. I'm surprised you still like her. Don't you remember all the times she's made you the butt of her jokes."

"To be fair I think that might just be her humor."

"Jokes are only funny if everyone is laughing together. Not if everyone is laughing at one person."

"You are very wise."

"I had a pretty decent big sister. So what did Jessica do this time?"

"She got into Em's head a little bit."

"Yikes. What did she say to her?"

"Just that she doesn't see the two of us fitting together."

"Well, that's just ridiculous. You're both adults, it's up to you to decide where you fit in each other's lives."

"Exactly."

"Out of curiosity, where does Em fit into your life?"

"Not you, too."

"Hey, Em is my best friend, and you are my sister. I couldn't be more excited that the two people I love most in the world are giving love a chance. That being said, I'm more than a little invested in this not being a terrible failure." Jamie said, his tone serious.

"Okay, I guess. In all fairness I don't know the exact answer. I don't know why things with Em work as well as they do. But it's like we just fit. She's this missing piece I didn't know I needed for my puzzle. We haven't been dating even a month, but I miss her when she's not here. That's all I know."

"Awww, sis, I'm going to cry."

"Oh, stop it. I don't know what we're going to be for one another, but I could see this being the start to something really special for both of us."

"Sis!" Jamie said in his loudest sweetest tone of voice. His range was ear piercingly high. Devon knew he meant it, she could feel his excitement through the phone.

This really could be the beginning of something special for both of them. Devon's heart lurched. The feeling that grew deep inside her was a strange one. The longing for the start of a new adventure with Em, mixed with a feeling of familiarity. How strange, for something to feel like the start of a new adventure and to be as familiar as coming home at the same time.

Chapter 13

Em finished hanging orange and purple lights up in Natural Wonders. Something about Halloween always invigorated her. Most people probably didn't see it as the start of something. People associated Spring with new beginnings. But Em always saw Fall as the time for preparation for new things, Winter as the time to clear old things away, the Spring was the time of new things being brought about. But it all started with Fall, and nothing was more reminiscent of the time of year than Halloween.

This year she had decorated the shop up like the inside of an old fortune teller's tent. Obviously, she wouldn't be doing any readings on children. But she would take any excuse to bring out her giant crystal balls. Violet, who was more like the mascot of Natural Wonders than she was the manager, also loved this time of year. The old woman was practically gliding through the store. Violet was dressed in the same costume she wore every year. She liked to say she was the old witch from Hansel and Gretel. Regardless, Violet had made Natural Wonders a favorite stop for all the kids celebrating Halloween. Every year, Violet would dress up and read scary stories to the kids who came by, a favorite for both the kids and the parents.

The story times made the customers happy, which in turn made Emilia happy. Every year they dressed in matching witches outfits. Violet had provided the costumes and Em had always been enthralled by them. Hers was made of heavy midnight blue fabric, with black lace overlay.

"So is your new friend still coming tonight to help with the candy?" Violet grinned and her eyes sparkled.

"Which friend? I have two coming tonight," Em answered coyly.

"I hope they don't get jealous of one another."

"Me, too. Especially since they're related. I would hate to start a family feud."

"Nonsense, you haven't lived any life at all until you've had at least two members of the same family fighting over you," Violet said with a little too much conviction. It was enough fervor to get Em to turn her head. Sometimes Violet made her wonder.

"I'm here," Jamie said, bursting through the door.

"Oh, look who it is," Violet said, her face lighting up. There was something about Jamie that had an almost magnetic effect on the woman.

"Ahhh, where's my favorite?" Jamie didn't get a chance to finish. Violet had wrapped him up in her arms. They were the picture of contrast. Jamie was tall and slender, being crushed by Violet who was short and wide.

"Has my sister come yet?" Jamie managed to choke out.

"Not yet. She had to get some stuff done at the school." Jamie nodded. Violet finally released her grip and Em watched as her friend almost crumpled to the floor. There was a sweetness to the interactions between Violet and Jamie. Violet had never married and had never had children, a fact she was most proud of. Having survived untethered in an era when the life path for most women was so clearly defined. Still, Em knew there was a part of Violet that saw her, and Jamie as family. Em felt the same way about the older woman. After her aunt had passed Violet was there for her in a way even Em's own parents seemed incapable of.

The bell above the door chimed once more as Devon stepped through. A light drizzle of rain had begun to fall outside, Devon shook herself adjusting to the warmth of the store. She took off her red scarf and jacket, hanging them on a peg near the door. Her red hair was warm as flames against the contrast of her skin.

"Hey there, Sunshine," Em called up to her. Devon's strides made up the space between them quickly. She wrapped her arms around Em.

"Sunshine?" Devon asked. Em allowed herself to sink deeper into the embrace. Devon's scent was warm vanilla and cinnamon, it took Em back to her childhood. To those holiday mornings by her aunt's fireplace with cookies baking in the kitchen.

"It just came to me," Em said with a shrug.

"I like it," Devon said, brushing a kiss against Em's cheek.

"No hello for your baby brother?" Jamie chortled. Devon and Em each rolled their eyes.

"Oh no, see that right there? You two can't gang up on me. I can't take double the eye rolls in my life." Devon and Em each broke into laughter.

"But sometimes you're so eye roll worthy," Devon snickered, giving her brother a hug.

"Rude," Jamie declared. They all laughed.

"Did you bring your costumes?" Violet asked both Devon and Jamie pointedly.

"Of course." They each answered briskly. It was one of those times that their resemblance to one another showed through. Em took a moment to really study them both, from the curve of their lips and shape of their eyes it was clear they were related. Violet just grabbed them both by the hands as if they were children and escorted them to the bathrooms. When Devon emerged she was no longer Devon. She was Red Riding Hood. When Jamie emerged he was himself, just with a more glittery top and black dancing pants.

"Whoa, that outfit is...." Looking at Devon, Em struggled to find the words she was looking for. The hood she wore was a heavy velvet in the perfect crimson color. Devon's red hair provided the perfect highlight for the crimson hood.

"You like it?" Devon asked.

"It's amazing," Em said.

"I borrowed it from a friend in the theater department. When I saw it I knew it would be perfect," Devon said with a squeal.

"I'm sorry, but what about me?" Jamie gasped.

"You look great too, friend," Em said with a smile.

The bell at the front of the store rang signifying the first visitors of the night. A group of five children came in all dressed in various costumes of witches, and werewolves. There were even a couple of zombies and vampires. Em knew the parents as they were regulars to the store. She let Jamie and Violet greet the children, while she spoke with the parents. Devon's hand was grabbed by two little girls who insisted she sit with them for story time. Em watched as Devon's face lit up, she happily talked about her costume and asked them about theirs. In times like these Em could tell the difference between herself, being an only child and people raised with a sibling.

The night was a constant buzz of movement. A perfectly choreographed dance of Devon greeting the children, taking them to Violet, and Jamie and Em making small talk with her customers. The mechanics just worked perfectly with everyone falling into their roles naturally. Em stole the occasional glance at Devon, she was amazing, so warm and welcoming to everyone that came through the doors. Devon didn't have to be here for this she had chosen to be, Em reminded herself. On more than one occasion when Em stole a glance of Devon she found it returned. Their eye contact, deep even from across the room, threatened to pull them together.

The hours passed quickly for Em. Being surrounded by her favorite people and loyal customers made for the perfect evening. By eight o'clock the stream of visitors had stopped. The cold Fall weather meant that parents were taking their kids back home for bedtime. Devon gave a long stretch, her arms over her head.

"This has been so fun," Devon said, with a half yawn.

"You need to get going?" Em asked.

"I have an early class," Devon said almost apologetically.

"I understand. I'll walk you to the door," Em said, taking Devon's hand in her own. Her hand was warm and soft, Em liked the way Devon curled her fingers around hers.

They stopped at the coat peg in the front of the store. Devon pulled on her jacket then stood staring at the empty coat peg.

"Is everything alright?" Em asked after a moment.

"Not really. I could have sworn I left my scarf right here. But it's gone." Devon said with a tremor starting to enter her voice. Em walked over searching the area around the coat peg desperately for the scarf. The red scarf was nowhere to be found. From across the room Jamie noted his sister wringing her hands with worry and came over.

"Hey, sis, what's going on?"

"I lost my red scarf," Devon said.

"The one Grandma made you?" Jamie asked.

"Yeah." Devon's voice seemed very small.

"Well, let's look around the store. Who knows, maybe it got moved somehow." Devon nodded. They all searched every inch of the shop, even the bathrooms but had no success. It was clear to Em that what had most likely occurred was that one of her customers grabbed the scarf by mistake. Of course, on a night when so many of her customers had visited, finding the right one would be a hard task.

"Sis, I think someone else probably took it home by accident. I'm sorry. I'm sure they'll realize it and bring it back," Jamie said finally. Devon's shoulders slumped and her hair covered her face. Her expression was a far cry from the happiness she had expressed earlier. It broke Em's heart to see her that way. She wrapped her arms around Devon.

"We'll find it, don't worry," Em said, trying her best to soothe Devon.

"Sure. Thank you for trying. I should get going," Devon said, giving Em one final squeeze before heading out the door.

"I'm going to walk with her," Jamie said, excusing himself. Em nodded. She sat in a chair behind the counter and thought to herself.

"Anything I can do to help?" Violet asked. An idea occurred to Em and her eyes locked with Violet's.

"Can you get me some paper and a pen?" Em asked. Violet got a gleam in her blue eyes and gave a nod.

Em wrote down the names of every single customer she could remember seeing that night. She handed Violet the list.

"Can you think of anyone else who came tonight?" She asked. Violet studied the list up close and gave a shake of her head.

"Nope. That's a good list. What's next?" Violet asked.

"Next, I ask for a little guidance and make my way through the list."

Em closed her eyes tight and lifted her finger. *"This is the name of the person who accidentally took Devon's scarf tonight."* Em said the words out loud then brought her finger down to the paper. The name her finger covered was Amy and Steve McGreggor. They were a nice couple who had been coming into her store for years with their three year-old. Their son Ian loved looking at her rocks and crystals.

"Now what?" Violet asked, half intrigued, half confused.

"I guess I call them. It's nine on a Saturday. Hopefully, everyone is still awake," Em said. Violet shook her head.

"Wouldn't you rather wait until morning?" Violet asked. The sadness written on Devon's face flashed across Em's memory. She shook her head and pulled out her cell. Violet patted her on the arm and began tidying up the store. Em took in a deep breath and dialed the number.

Chapter 14

Devon sat in her living room hugging one of her couch pillows. Her mood had turned sour. *How could she have been so thoughtless?* Surely she could have put her grandma's scarf in Em's backroom, somewhere away from everyone else's things. It hadn't even occurred to her to ask Em to put the scarf somewhere special, somehow that made her feel even worse. Jamie had walked her home; given her a hug, some encouraging words then left. Her brother never could stand to see her sad.

Lights in the driveway told her that a car was pulling in. Perfect. With her luck she would lose her scarf and be murdered by a serial killer on the same night. She toyed with the tiny luck jar in her hand. It was special because Em had made it, but it didn't feel particularly lucky at the present moment. A knock at the door startled her, even if it was expected.

"Who is it?" Devon called out. She wasn't entirely sure she wanted to invest the time in leaving the couch.

"It's Em. Can I come in? It's really starting to rain out here."

Devon let go of her reluctance and rushed to the door. Em ran inside, rain dripping from her hair and jacket.

"Oh, my god, come in. Take off that jacket, you're going to freeze." Devon said. Em's arm was tucked carefully inside the jacket. When she pulled her arm out Devon was surprised to see her scarf in Em's hand. Em gave her the scarf peeling off her wet jacket.

"Wait. How did you? Where was it?" The questions poured out of Devon quicker than Em could answer, she waited for her to stop talking before she responded.

"A family that comes to the store fairly often grabbed it from the peg by mistake. I made a list of all the customers I knew that came in and narrowed it down."

"I can't believe you found it. And that you went through so much trouble on my behalf."

"What? Of course I went through trouble on your behalf. You're my..." Her words trailed off. Devon knew Em wasn't sure how to finish, but she wanted to hear her answer.

"I'm your what?" Devon asked almost too gently. Her voice so soft that she was afraid Em wouldn't be able to hear her. Em locked eyes with her, eyes two glowing green embers in the night.

"You're my person," Em said with so much sureness in her tone it knocked Devon off guard. She took a beat to look inside herself, examining. Devon knew almost immediately that her own feelings mirrored Em's exactly.

"You're my person, too," Devon said, closing the distance between them. She took Em by the hand and pulled her to the couch, wrapping her up in a blanket. Devon pulled Em close. Em lay her head against Devon's neck, nuzzling her there. She laughed at the tickling sensation.

"What are you doing?" Devon asked.

"I just want to bury my face in your fur," Em said with a smile. She kissed Devon on the neck. Devon felt a rush of heat spread across her body. Her finger rested under Em's face, tilting it upward until their eyes met.

"I adore you. Do you know that?" Devon said.

"You do?" Em asked, her head tilting to the side.

"Of course I do. I'm crazy about you. And I think those feelings are only going to grow after tonight. I mean you went out and found my scarf, on a rainy night, just so I wouldn't be sad. You're, amazing."

"If you keep this up I'm going to start hiding your scarf just so I can find it again," Em teased.

"Em, I'm serious, I just want you to know that I think you're amazing."

"Hey, I do know. Because you show me in a million little ways," Em said, her tone taking on a note of seriousness.

"Well good. Because this. No one has ever cared for me this way. No one has ever gone out of their way to do something just because they knew I was sad and they wanted to make me happy. And I know we could say it's just a scarf. But not to me. To me it's the last piece of my grandma. I wear it because I like to feel like she's close to me. Tonight when we couldn't find it, I really thought it was gone for good. Thank you so much for finding it."

"Aww, sunshine. There's very little I wouldn't do to make you happy," Em said, pulling Devon in for a passionate kiss. Outside there was a loud clap of thunder. Devon's lights went dark. In spite of herself Devon let out a little whimper and felt Em's arms encircle her.

"It's okay, just the storm," Em whispered, her voice cutting through the darkness.

"Right, of course," Devon said, trying to sound more sure

of herself than she felt.

"Do you have any flashlights?" Em suggested. Devon shook her head, then realized Em couldn't see her.

"I don't, but I do have candles and a lighter," Devon offered.

"That will do the trick. Come on, let's get some lit before I go," Em said. Devon was struck by the word *go*. How could one little word set her so ill at ease?

They gathered as many candles as they could find from Devon's pantry, lighting them. Em's face was lit by the strange glow of the candles. A beautiful thing carved out in the darkness.

"There you go. You're all set for the night," Em's smile widened, providing Devon with more warmth than the candles.

"Thank you." Devon pulled Em in close. She liked the way their bodies fit together. Enjoyed the feel of Em's hand in her own.

"I know this is a strange request, but could you stay? Things always seem so much worse in the dark," Devon said. As soon as the words left her, she felt silly. What kind of grown woman needs someone to stay with her during a blackout?

"Actually, that would be great. It's getting late and it would be nice to just stay in for the rest of the night. Plus it's raining," Em said. Devon pulled her in closer, whispering against her ear.

"I wouldn't want you to get wet. Unless I'm the one turning you on," Devon felt a shiver run through Em's body.

"Devon," Em's voice came out as a whimper. Devon took Em by the hand.

"Come upstairs. Let's get you out of those wet clothes and into bed with me," Devon said. Em followed her willingly up the stairs and to her bedroom by the light of a candle. Devon pulled some warm clothes out of her closet for Em to put on. Devon lay in her bed and waited, when Em came she slid the covers back. Em climbed in beside her, providing an extra dose of warmth. Devon wrapped an arm around Em's waist and her head against her chest. Em played with Devon's hair, allowing the strands to slip through her fingers.

"Did you mean what you said downstairs?" Devon asked. In the near darkness, her voice sounded too loud.

"Which part?" Em asked with a yawn.

"The part about me being your person?" Devon asked.

"I did mean it. We've only recently come back into each other's lives, but you're very important to me," Em said.

"Did you mean it when you said I was your person, too?" Em asked.

"Of course. Like you said this whole thing is new. But I already can't picture my life without you in it. All I know is that I like having you close." Devon gave Em's body a squeeze with her arm.

"I feel the same way. I think you and I will be in each other's lives for a long time," Em said, her green eyes bright in the candle's light.

"Is that a psychic twinge?" Devon asked.

"Maybe." Em smiled.

"But it's also what my heart is telling me," Em said.

"Your heart told you that?" Devon asked.

"My heart tells me that every time I look at you." Em gave Devon the sweetest of kisses on the top of her head. They snuggled in together, each enjoying the closeness of the other's body. Sleep tugged at both of them, until Devon felt herself drift away.

Chapter 15

Em made what she hoped was the final lap around her home. She couldn't find her favorite Oracle deck of tarot cards. Today was the big Fall festival and she had agreed to give psychic readings in one of the booths. A gesture Em couldn't imagine making prior to Devon coming into her life. Devon sat sprawled out on her couch, she wore a bemused smile on her face.

"I'm glad you're finding this entertaining," Em said with a pout.

"Oh, babe, I'm not laughing at you. Come over here and tell me what's bothering you," Em walked over and sank to the couch.

"It's just been a long time. What if no one is interested in hearing what I have to say? What if I don't know what to say?"

"Hey, you're going to be amazing. No one psychics like you do." Em burst into laughter.

"Did you just use psychic as a verb?"

"I did. And I stand by it," Devon remarked. She reached behind her and brought out the tarot deck Em had been looking for.

"Is this what you were looking for?" Devon asked coyly. The smirk on her face brought a heat to Em's core. She tried desperately to force the feeling back down. Getting through the day would be hard enough without Devon on the brain.

It had been a week since the night Em had brought Devon her scarf. They had spent every night together since. Devon could still cause Em's body to quake. Thoughts of her could still make her mind race. After spending so much time together Emilia had been afraid that they might get too comfortable. Had been afraid that the magic between them might dwindle. Instead, the opposite was proving true. Em was more enthralled by Devon every time they went home together. Her heart pounded with anticipation when she knew they were going to see one another. Saying she had a crush or that she was smitten just didn't do the feelings she had justice. Em was falling on her face head over heels. She was "rush for the moon and wish on a star" in love with Devon.

Em gave Devon a fast kiss across the cheek. A kiss any longer and she risked getting pulled into other pursuits. Devon stood, she fluffed out her hair and walked towards the door. When she got there she stopped, holding her hand out for Em.

"Are you ready?" Devon asked.

"I'm ready," Em said, taking Devon's hand in her own she felt her nerves melt away.

Nightshade University had been transformed into a spectacular display of Fall. Pumpkins lined the sidewalks, ghosts made of sheets hung from the trees. A black cat scurried in front of Em as she walked, she took it decidedly as a good omen.

Up ahead Em spotted Quinn and Jessica. Tensions were still running high between Devon and Jessica, so Em knew she would need to navigate those interactions with care.

"Em you made it," Jessica said, her tone overly excited.

"I promised to be here. Natural Wonders is happy to support the community," Em said, pointing to her Nightshade University sweatshirt.

"I love your spirit," Quinn said, her smile genuine. She took Em by the arm and led her towards the tents of local vendors.

"I'll take Em to her tent," Quinn said to Jessica. When they had walked down the sidewalk she whispered to Em.

"I hope that was okay. Things have been stressful between Jessica and Devon. The last thing you need is her trying to get you on her side," Quinn remarked.

"Thanks, that is absolutely the last thing I'm interested in today."

Quinn directed her to a tent which had a sign at the front that read:

Natural Wonders: Psychic Readings will be offered by Emilia Thorne.

"What do you think?" Quinn asked. Em looked at the silver lettering against a midnight blue sign and smiled.

"It's perfect." Em said. Quinn gave her a quick smile before rushing off. Em sat in her booth and began unpacking her products from Natural Wonders. She didn't wait long, a group of three girls swung by for their free readings. Em enjoyed speaking to them. They listened intently as she drew her tarot cards and gave their readings. Each girl bought a crystal bracelet, saying they would be for their friendship.

The sound of a cat meowing surprised her. She looked past the table and saw the same black cat staring back at her. The cat jumped up to the table.

"Hello there, are you going to stay for a while? Because you would really be great for my overall aesthetic," Em said, reaching out her hand. The cat bumped her hand with its head then lay on the table purring. Em stared admiringly at the feline.

"I think you're going to be my new mascot," she teased.

Several students came by for their readings. Em chatted with each student, she gave readings or recommended crystals. An hour came and went fairly quickly. Devon arrived a short time later, out of breath. She held a fist full of brochures in her hand. On her sweater she wore a large name tag.

"Hey there, sunshine, nice of you to come visit," Em teased.

"I know, I'm sorry. I tried to get away sooner. They just have me so busy out there." Devon leaned over the table to give Em a kiss. Annoyed by the interruption the cat gave a begrudging meow. Devon startled.

"Holy shit! Wait a minute, did you get a cat?"

"Of course not. The cat seems to have adopted my table though." Em grinned. On her belt a walkie talkie chirped to life.

"Devon. Are you there?" The voice was Jessica's. Devon gave a moan before hitting the answer button.

"I'm here, Jessica. What's up?"

"I need to see you by the food tents," Jessica demanded.

"I'll head right over," Devon said, her tone dripping in sarcasm. Em couldn't help but giggle. Sarcasm was so far from Devon's typical demeanor that it was funny to witness.

"Duty calling?" Em teased.

"Yes, duty disguised as Jessica," Devon retorted.

"I'm sure she just wants to talk logistics," Em said.

"One can only hope," Devon said. She excused herself, giving the cat one solid scratch behind the ears before darting down the sidewalk. Em watched Devon go.

"I guess it's just you and me," she said to the cat. The cat stared up at her, with golden eyes that were completely disinterested.

More groups of college kids came as the day progressed. The day began to fade to evening. Quinn stopped by to check in.

"How are things?"

"Pretty great actually. I've given quite a few readings and I've sold out of most of the bracelets and some of my crystals."

"Somehow, I knew your booth was going to be popular." Quinn smiled. She rubbed her hands against her jeans, Em got the sense that she wanted something.

"Do you want a reading?" Em offered.

"Umm, I would love one. But would it be too much trouble? I know you're probably getting ready to close down."

"I am but I think I can squeeze in one more. Come on in." Em gestured for Quinn to come inside, she closed the flaps of the tent for some privacy. She began to cut her deck sliding her cards through her hands. Quinn had an unmistakeably nervous expression on her face. The first card that fell was the devil, not always a good way to start.

By the end of the reading Emilia was confused, though Quinn seemed to be taking everything in stride. She thanked Em before rushing off. The cat seemed to look at her with its piercing gold eyes in accusation.

"I don't know what you wanted me to do about it," Em said, shrugging her shoulders. The cat gave a yawn as she stretched. Em decided the best thing she could do was to go find

Devon.

"If you're still here when I get back, I'm going to assume you're homeless. Then I'm going to take you to my place until I can take you to get scanned by the vet. The cat purred; Em scratched her behind the ears. She trotted down the same sidewalk she had watched Devon walk down earlier.

Chapter 16

Devon had started the day off with a low threshold for dealing with Jessica's bullshit. That level had dropped significantly in the hours since her arrival to Fall Fest. The event was wrapping up and Jessica had spent the day ordering Devon to do every menial task she could think of. Devon had swept leaves from all the major walkways, she had delivered lunch to the *new students'* section of the festival, and she had worked the mechanical bull while the regular operator took a lunch. As evening approached Devon was more than ready for the day to be over. The one redeeming event of the day was seeing Stuart arrive with a date. One less person's shit to deal with.

"Hey Devon, how did it go today?" Jessica's voice was nails across a chalkboard to Devon.

"It was fine," Devon said simply. The chances of Devon getting sucked into a conversation with Jessica were zero. She couldn't imagine any interaction with the other woman going well.

"Oh, come on, Devon. We need to talk. You stopped returning my texts and you only give one-word answers when we're around each other. What's that about?" Jessica asked, her face the picture of innocence.

"Seriously? Don't play innocent, Jessica, we've known each other too long for that. You know I'm still mad about you trying to put doubts in Em's head. And before you say anything, I'm not over here telling Jake about how petty you can be. I'm not telling the one good guy you've ever dated how maybe he should look twice before he falls in love with you." She spit the words out fast and harshly.

"The two situations are not similar at all. You have a tendency to promise forever only to bail on the other person. Honestly, Em should have doubts."

"What the literal fuck are you even talking about right now? I haven't even been back in town until recently."

"You know I'm talking about Brent."

"Brent? Are you kidding me? Brent was my high school boyfriend. Almost no one ends up with their high school sweetheart."

"You promised him you would stay in town with him.

Then you just left."

"I was in high school. Would I maybe handle that situation better if it came up today, sure. But you can't base all my relationships around what happened with Brent. Besides, he obviously went on and lived his life. Brent is fine," Devon said, her irritation growing by the minute.

"Fine? Devon, you weren't here. You didn't see the heartbreak he went through. He almost failed out of his freshman year, almost got kicked off the football team."

"How is that my fault?"

"He couldn't pull himself together after you left."

"Or maybe when we were together, I had to be the one to make sure he made it to class and practice. Maybe once I was gone he had to grow the fuck up. Maybe me leaving was the best thing to ever happen to him because he had to figure out how to do life for himself."

"Wow, Devon, that's pretty heartless. Brent was sad. He moped around for months trying to forget you. Everyone here tried to pull him out of it, I know I tried. Nothing worked. Meanwhile, you just got to run off and live your life. Carefree," Jessica said, her irritation clearly beginning to match Devon's.

"I'm not going to apologize for leaving my hometown or my high school boyfriend. It was the right decision for me. That doesn't have anything to do with Em. Or my relationship with her. I care about her." Devon threw her hands in the air, completely flustered.

"You like her now, but what happens when you get the urge to leave again?"

"Oh, my god! Where is this coming from?"

"I don't know Em well. But I do like her. I just think she deserves better than to be discarded by you the next time you get the urge to leave Nightshade."

"I'm not leaving Nightshade, and I'm not discarding Em. We don't even have a label yet. Seems a little premature to be arguing about me breaking Em's heart one day."

"You may not have a label but the woman is clearly smitten with you."

"Oh, my god, Jessica! Em and I are two adults enjoying one another's company. We're just having fun. It's not a significant relationship." Behind her, Devon heard a tiny gasp. She turned, already knowing what she was likely to find. Her fears were quickly confirmed. Em stood her face twisted. Her eyes brimmed with tears, she turned before Devon could watch them fall. Jessica and her dumb words were suddenly inconsequential. The only thing that mattered was Em.

Devon walked towards Em, laying a hand on her shoulder. Em shrugged the hand off. Her pace sped as Em tried walking away. Devon had to jog to keep up with her, finally grabbing Em's arm with a bit more firmness.

"Em, please stop. I want to talk to you. It's not what you think."

"I heard everything I needed to hear from you. I've been thinking of forever but it turns out this isn't even significant for you." Em's lip quivered with the words. Devon felt her heart breaking. No, not breaking. Breaking was too easy a word for what she felt inside. Her heart was ripping apart from the inside. Em ran off and Devon let a curse slip from her lips. Fuck!

She turned only to see Jessica standing there. Jessica had watched the whole scene unfold, that made the entire thing worse.

"Not one word from you." She warned, knowing that of course there would likely be several words.

"Oh, this isn't on me. You did this all on your own."

"You've been pushing me all day long."

"I didn't choose your words," Jessica reminded her. Devon wanted to lash out, but Jessica was right. She had spoken all on her own.

"I really like her," Devon said, her voice almost a plea. Jessica cocked her head and gave her a genuinely thoughtful look.

"If you like her, don't stand here yelling at me. We've known each other over a decade. We've been angry and happy and every other emotion with each other. You can always scream at me later. But if you don't want her to get away you should run after her now." Devon took a moment to give Jessica a nod of the head. Whatever else they were to each other, that had been genuinely good advice.

She began running down the sidewalk, almost colliding with Jamie. Her brother tried waving her down to stop. Devon kept going, running at full speed. In her mind she ran through what she needed to say to Em. An apology was obviously called for, but what would Em say? Up ahead she could see Em getting into her car. Devon's heart pounded inside her chest. This was the moment she had been running for, but now her throat tightened. Her mouth went dry and her thoughts ran so fast she wasn't sure what she should say. All she could hope was that Em would forgive her.

Chapter 17

Em's breath caught in her throat making it even harder to run. Hot tears stung her eyes. When she reached the tent everything was gone except for the cat.

"If you want to come with me, I'm leaving now," she directed. For once she was glad that she and Devon had driven separately. Em was surprised when she reached her car and saw that the cat had trailed behind her the entire way. Once the car door opened the cat jumped in, making itself comfortable on the passenger side. She would take him by the vet tomorrow to get scanned for a chip.

Devon's words still rung stinging her ears. *It's not a significant relationship.* That sentence had hurt. Nothing about her feelings for Devon had been insignificant and she had thought that was mutual. She wound back the clock of her memory, poring over moments. Dissecting all of Devon's words and actions. Looking for any evidence in her actions that would have made it obvious that things between them were more one-sided. What had she missed?

Emilia had just shoved the last box in her car when she heard someone screaming her name. Not just someone, Devon. Em turned and caught sight of Devon running at full speed towards her. At first, her inclination was to jump in her car. She wanted to run, to avoid whatever conversation Devon wanted to have. That inclination was overruled by her growing anger. She stood her ground waiting for Devon to reach her.

Devon got there sweaty and out of breath, but still easily the most beautiful woman in the world. Em hated that, even angry she found Devon attractive.

"Thanks for waiting. Holy shit, that was farther than I thought it was."

"What do you want Devon?" Em's tone and demeanor flustered Devon, she rubbed the back of her neck with a hand.

"I wanted to talk to you," Devon said, her voice unsure.

"Great, go ahead and say whatever you want to say," Em said, her voice raw with pain.

"You don't know what you walked in on. You came midway through the conversation with Jessica. I know how what you heard sounded."

"Oh, how did it sound?"

"It probably sounded like I don't value our relationship. Which you have to know isn't true."

"Do I? Because that's not what you said. You said we were just fun. You said this isn't a significant relationship."

"I didn't mean it that way."

"What I know is that you had a chance to stand up for our relationship and you chose to downplay it instead."

"Em, I hurt you and I'm sorry. All I meant was that we're having fun together, and we haven't made any promises to each other."

"I understand that you've been frustrated with Jessica. And I know that we haven't made any promises to one another. But you made me feel like I'm not important to you. Your words hurt me and they made me feel like this is some kind of frivolous fling for you. And maybe for you it is, but my feelings for you were real and deep. So I'm going to need you to figure out what this is for you, what I am to you. Because I can't be in a relationship with someone I'm not on the same page with." Em opened her car door, hopped in and drove off. Devon stood staring but she made no move to stop her.

Em could still see Devon watching her car from her rearview mirror. The only place she could think to go was Natural Wonders. That was her safe haven, the place that always made sense even when nothing did. She had spent days at a time there after she had finished the refurbishments. Those months after the death of her aunt had been hard, Natural Wonders had made it less so.

Violet still sat behind the counter. She had offered to work the day while Em handled the stand on campus. Em put the black cat down, and it ran immediately to Violet, meowing the whole way.

"Hello, there," Violet said, giving the cat a scratch when it jumped up to the counter. Then studying Em she nodded her head.

"I'm going to put some tea on. Would you like some?" Violet asked.

"Make mine a double," Em said. She wandered to the store's book section and sank into one of the velvet chairs. The feeling of being one hundred years old hit her. She stared at the books and at nothing in particular. Violet brought a cup of tea, sitting it on the table beside her. Em let the mug warm her hands.

"Thank you." Em said.

"Are you going to tell me why your face is so long? You were so happy yesterday."

"That was yesterday, a lot has happened in between." Em stared ahead; her eyes focused on nothing.

"So tell me about it," Violet urged.

"I walked in on a conversation between Devon and her friend Jessica. I wasn't meant to hear it."

"But you did, and Devon said something that upset you?"

"Yeah," Em said.

"So what did she say?"

"She said we were just fun. She said we aren't a significant relationship."

"Ouch," Violet said simply. She took a seat in the other velvet chair, opposite Em's.

"Ouch indeed," Em said, taking a sip of tea.

"Did she say anything to you?"

"Lots of things. None of them meant much to me. I don't

want to be her fling, or something new for her to try out."

"I don't think you are. It's clear she adores you. Perhaps she just chose her words poorly. Or maybe she didn't realize until now that you meant more to her."

"Maybe. But I'm not waiting around, hoping she figures it out."

"There's nothing wrong with asking for clarification," Violet said. Em nodded simply, her thoughts taking her elsewhere. Her phone buzzed, a missed text from Jamie flashed across the screen.

"Shit. I forgot I have plans with Jamie tonight."

"You could always tell him you're sick," Violet suggested.

"I don't lie to him. He's my best friend."

"From where I sit it doesn't sound like a lie. You're heart sick. Hurts just as bad if not worse than any physical ailment."

"Violet, you're very insightful today."

"I'm insightful everyday."

"Why don't I usually notice?"

"I usually just keep it to myself, " Violet said with a subtle smile. Em braced herself for the hundreds of response texts she was likely to get from Jamie. Once she opened that door, there would be no going back.

Chapter 18

Devon felt as if someone had punched her in the gut. Not just anyone, but Em. She wasn't sure what she'd expected from Em. Had she expected immediate forgiveness? Devon's shoulders slouched and she stared at her shoes as she walked. Her brain was a fog of swirling illusive thoughts. As soon as she grabbed hold of a thought, it evaporated and led her to another.

"Devon, slow down." She immediately recognized the voice of her brother behind her and stopped.

"Where are you even going?" Jamie asked. He stood in front of her hands placed on her shoulders. Devon felt so tired, she leaned forward resting her head against his chest. He smelled of deep wooded forests, it was a different smell than Devon was used to from her brother.

"Hey, is everything okay?"

"No," Devon said simply.

"Well, would you like to talk about it?" Jamie asked, his

voice half of a tease.

"Maybe," Devon said, face still buried in her brother's chest.

"I didn't get that. Come over here. Let's sit down and talk everything out." Jamie took her hand and led her to a row of benches that had been set up for the students. Devon followed her brother, plopping to the nearest bench.

"So tell me what's going on," Jamie said.

"Em and I had a fight. It's my fault and I think I really fucked up. I think this could have ended things with us." Jamie was obviously practicing restraint. His eyebrow lifted a fraction and she could see him start to worry his lower lip.

"Why don't you start from the beginning?" Jamie offered.

"You know how Jessica really made me angry a while back?"

"Yeah, she said something to Em that made her question things with the two of you."

"Exactly. Well, today she's had me running a million tiny errands. Then basically wanted to talk out our issues."

"Bad timing, but I would expect nothing less."

"Yeah. So we get into this whole talk. And Jessica is saying that I left Brent brokenhearted, and she doesn't want to see the same thing happen to Em. And I just kind of snapped."

"Okay, what did you say?"

"Basically just that she didn't know what she was talking about. I said that Em and I are just having fun… and that what we have isn't a significant relationship. I was just so angry with her, and I wanted to drop the whole talk. It would have been fine but Em overheard everything."

"Ouch, Devon, I mean that was a harsh thing to say. And I'm sure it was hard for Em to hear."

"Yeah, it didn't go well. Em ran off and I chased after her. I apologized but Em said that I had a chance to stand up for what we were and instead I denied that it meant anything."

"Yikes. Yeah you fucked up."

"Thanks, Jamie. I thought you were going to try and make me feel better?"

"Okay, you're right you fucked up. But the good news is I don't think it's something that Em can't forgive you for."

"You really think she might be able to forgive me?"

"Em has put up with me as her best friend, for like a million years. Her capacity for forgiveness is pretty vast." Devon chuckled.

"The hurt is fresh for her right now. And if you were going to push a button, that's a pretty vulnerable spot for her. But it sounds like what she really wants is to know that her feelings for you are reciprocated."

"They definitely are. I can't think of anyone that I've felt like this about."

"That's a good start," Jamie said with a smile.

"Ugh, I just wish Jessica hadn't made me so angry. If she would have just backed off this never would have happened."

"If you want Em to forgive you, that is going to have to stop."

"What's going to have to stop?"

"Blaming Jessica. You have to stop that."

"What do you mean? If she hadn't gotten under my skin none of this would have happened."

"Maybe that's true. It probably is. But Em isn't going to

see it that way. Em is going to say Jessica is responsible for her part in the whole encounter. But that the words you said were your own. She's going to expect you to take ownership for the part you played in this." Jamie's words poked the bruise forming around Devon's heart. Devon swallowed hard, allowing herself to take in the truth of her brother's words. The fact was Jessica hadn't hurt Em, she had. No one had picked her words for her. As such, she was the one to blame for the hurt Em was feeling. The realization threatened to crush Devon under the weight.

"What do you think I should do?" Devon asked Jamie.

"Give her a little time. Send her flowers tomorrow. Ask her to talk. I've seen the two of you together. You're both so smitten with each other. I truly believe you can work things out with one another."

"Is that just wishful thinking on your part? Or do you really think Em could forgive me?"

"Can it be a little bit of both? I do think Em will forgive you, and I am putting all my wishful thinking powers into it."

"Thanks, Jamie. You really are sort of the best brother ever."

"I really am. You're lucky to have me," Jamie said, teasing.

Devon gave him a light smack on the arm.

"This sucks. I hurt someone I really care about. I didn't want to do that."

"I know. Sometimes we hurt the people closest to us. It's an unfortunate part of humanity."

"I don't like it."

"The fact that it bothers you this much is why I know things are going to work out," Jamie said.

"You really have a lot of faith in this working out," Devon said, pinning him with a stare.

"I have all the faith in the world when it comes to you and Em. I would lay odds on this working out."

"I hope you're right," Devon said.

"You have to give her a chance to process. But I know she cares about you and that you care about her. So hopefully everything else can be worked out."

Devon couldn't stand sitting and talking about Em. Jamie seemed to understand she was going home. She stopped to send Em a text before she hopped in her car. The drive home was draining. Gone were the thoughts of what fun she and Em would be getting into later. It was just her, alone. It occurred to Devon that she hadn't had many nights without Em since they started seeing one another.

As soon as she pulled into her place she checked her phone. Hope against hope was crushed when she saw there was still no response to her text. Her home felt lonely, she put her keys down on the table. Her bed lay empty, Em's side was still disrupted from the morning.

Devon lay down and closed her eyes, but Em's scent still clung to her sheets and pillows. Em was a ghost lingering in her bed while still very much alive. She gave a frustrated huff, pulling Em's pillow close to her. Devon breathed deep, imagining the pillow was Em. A pillow was a poor substitute, it lacked the warmth of Em's body. The feel of it was wrong. Devon felt hot tears fall down her cheeks, and wished she could rewind the day.

Chapter 19

Em woke up sore and disoriented. It had been a long time since she had opted to sleep at the store. Her bed here was a small couch. The cushions were fluffy enough, but it was still a poor substitute for the bed she had back home. At the other end of the couch the black cat stared at her. Violet had agreed to pick the cat up that morning and take it to a local vet clinic to be scanned for a microchip. Since her arrival, the cat had hunted down five mice. Em had started calling her Artemis, a name fit for a hunter.

"Good morning Artemis," Em said to the cat. She had told Violet she would stay so she could get a jumpstart of inventory. Em suspected the older woman knew she stayed so that she didn't have to face her empty house, or her empty bed. Whether she liked it or not Devon had become a fixture in her life. Since their time together had started, spending a night alone had become rare. Em found herself missing Devon's presence, it made holding onto her anger hard.

A loud knocking at the front of the store pulled her the rest of the way off the couch. When she saw that it was Jamie, she wasn't surprised. She was shocked that he had settled for simple texting the night before, instead of a full-blown intervention. Em unlocked the door allowing her friend to come inside.

"I come bearing gifts," Jamie said, holding out a box of doughnuts. Em gave a small smile.

"Thank you," Em said, taking the doughnuts to the counter. She knew she didn't have to say more, Jamie would want to fill the silence.

"Right off the bat, I talked to Devon. She told me everything and I know that's probably why you didn't feel like going out last night. Which is fine, I totally understand that. Devon is my sister, but you're my best friend. I really wanted to make sure you're doing okay." The words spilled out of Jamie. Em cocked her head to the side, giving him a thoughtful glance. She opened the box of doughnuts and pulled one with sprinkles out.

"I'm going to be fine," Em said finally.

"Obviously, but I want to be here for you."

"I know you do, but this is different. Devon is your sister, I don't know if I should talk about this with you."

"But you talk to me about everything," Jamie said, his lips

turning to a pout.

"Everything that isn't about your sister."

"I can be impartial," Jamie said, moving a hand to cover his heart. Em pinned him with a look and shook her head.

"Fine, come on." Em took her doughnut over to the velvet chairs. Jamie followed, happy to be invited into her life.

"What did Devon say?" Em asked. Jamie gave her a strained look, but eventually broke.

"She said she fucked up. That she said some things that she regretted saying."

"Did she tell you that one of the things she said was that our relationship wasn't significant?"

"Yes, she told me," Jamie said simply. He took a bite of his doughnut letting the crumbs fall on his shirt.

"What the hell am I supposed to do with that Jamie?" Em asked.

"What do you mean?"

"I'm very invested in this relationship. My heart is all in, but maybe for Devon this is just a good time. She's got lots of friends and a big circle of people, maybe for her this only counts as a casual fling."

"You don't really think that," Jamie said almost too casually.

"I wonder about it," Em said. Jamie gave her a look and smiled.

"As her brother I can tell you that this thing between you is special for her."

"I don't know if I can trust that."

"Then trust me. I've seen my sister in relationships. This is special."

"Maybe, but does she know that it's special? Because it didn't sound like it yesterday."

"Look, I know it doesn't sound good. She shouldn't have said that, but her feelings are real. And I think your feelings are real too."

"Obviously, we wouldn't be sitting here if I didn't care at all."

"The question is are you ready to forgive her?"

"The answer is no. I need more than some frivolous words and gestures to prove she's actually in this. I'm not interested in investing my equity into something that doesn't mean that much to her."

"Em," Jamie whined.

"What? You say she's invested. Great! Let's see some proof that this is significant to her."

"But what does that mean?" Jamie asked.

"I don't know," Em admitted grumpily.

The bell above the shop door rang. A man stood in the doorway with an enormous bouquet of roses.

"Delivery for Emilia Thorne," the man said loudly. The flowers covered his face. Em walked over, her heart almost skipped a beat when she saw the arrangement. A romantic at heart, roses had always been her favorites. Em took the flowers from the man and set them on the counter. She read the card, *To Em, from Devon. I'm so sorry, please let me make this up to you.* The delivery man had Em sign for the flowers then scurried back to his truck.

"See this is a good start," Em said.

"Well then, I'm glad she took my advice." Jamie said, puffing out his chest.

"Wait a minute. You told her to send me flowers?" Em asked, her stare penetrating enough that it caused him to take a step back.

"I may have suggested it. But she definitely followed through all on her own."

"I don't know if that's enough," Em said, with a shrug of her shoulders.

"I think I just need to think about some things," Em said, the implication was clear. She needed some time to herself. Jamie, picked up on her hint immediately.

"Sure, I should get going. I just wanted to say one more thing."

"What's that?"

"Whatever happens between you and Devon, please can we still be friends?" A little piece of Em's heart broke off.

"Jamie, you've been my best friend for over a decade. You are always welcome in my life, no matter what happens with anyone else. I love you."

"Good, not that I was worried. But, it's still good to hear you say that." Em pulled him in for a hug. The gesture seemed to be enough, Jamie walked out with a smile.

Em crumpled onto the chair behind the counter. The roses sitting across from her seemed to be mocking her. She tried her best to gather her intuition, to find whatever she needed to know about Devon. But there was nothing. Where Devon was concerned her gifts proved to be useless. She was so smitten that it felt overpowering. The anger she felt mocked her. Em looked at the flowers again and decided she didn't like them after all, she dropped them into the trash.

In her mind the worst part was that she couldn't decide if she even had the right to be upset. Devon was correct, they had made no commitments to one another. And they were having a good time. Two adults having a mutually beneficial relationship wasn't a bad thing. So why was she upset? Devon had said that their relationship wasn't significant, and it had cut her, more than she cared to admit. Em looked down at the flowers in the trash can, the walls of her heart crumbled. She took them out and placed them back on the counter.

Chapter 20

Another department meeting meant more time Devon would never get back. Her days had passed so slowly over the past week. She had hoped Em would at least text her, but she hadn't received anything. Not even after sending flowers. Devon sank into her office chair, determined to answer all the student emails she had been putting off. A knock at her door caused her to stir, she glanced up and found Quinn there. The woman pinned her with a stare.

"Come on in," Devon said. Quinn walked in and sat in the extra chair usually reserved for students.

"Hey, I was just wondering what time Em was wanting us to come by for the Halloween party?" A knife slid through Devon's heart. She had almost forgotten that Em was throwing her annual Halloween party.

"I'm actually not sure," Devon said, her voice cracking.

"Hey, are you all right? I wanted to check in." Quinn asked, her eyes focusing uncomfortably on Devon.

"Check in about what?" Devon sighed.

"Check in about you, like as a person. Not business related." Devon shifted, uneasy in her chair.

"It's just that you've seemed pretty distracted this week. And a little... Well, you're a bit grumpy." Quinn threw her hands up in a defensive gesture. Devon forced a smile; she knew Quinn was right. She had found it hard to focus since her fight with Em.

"I'm sorry. I'm sure I have been off the last couple of days. It's just that Em and I had a fight." Quinn nodded her head, sympathetic. She and her ex had broken up then gotten back together almost too many times to count.

"I'm sorry I brought up the party, I didn't know. You and Em are really good together. I'm sure it'll work out," Quinn said smiling.

"Thanks. I hope so," Devon said. Inside, she had her doubts. There was only so much she could do if Em refused to even talk to her. That part hurt the most, the silence. Quinn excused herself leaving Devon alone once more with her thoughts. When she could take no more she messaged Jamie.

"Lunch?"

"I'm there." Jamie's response came almost immediately. He was definitely the responsive text*er* in the family.

She met him at Hooligans, a sandwich shop near the university. Her brother came in wearing a t-shirt and jeans with open-toed sandals.

"How are you wearing open-toed shoes? It's October."

"I just really wanted to." Devon had always loved her brother's take on life. For Jamie life was a magical adventure where he never knew what would happen next.

"So how are you doing, sis?" Jamie asked. His eyes studied her, taking in her appearance.

"I've been better. Em still hasn't responded to me. I'm not sure what to do with the silence. I don't know if this crosses any particular boundaries, but I need to know how Em is doing?" Devon asked.

"You're asking me how Em is doing?" Jamie asked.

"Yes, because I'm barely able to function."

"Honestly, Em is grumpy and miserable just like you are. I don't know if I can handle you both being in a bad mood at the same time. Between the two of you this whole break-up is ruining my life."

"Oh, I'm sorry that my heartbreak is inconveniencing you, bro."

"That isn't what I meant and you know it," Jamie said, folding his arms over his chest.

"I know it isn't but that's how you sounded."

"I'm sorry. It's just that I hate seeing you both in pain. And it feels like if the two of you would talk it out you'd be fine."

"Sure, but it's hard to talk it out with someone who refuses to answer my texts."

"Ugh, I know. I know. There's only so much you can do. And you're trying not to overwhelm her or be too aggressive. I don't know. It's just hard when a conversation obviously needs to happen. But the two people involved are just...." Jamie gestured to the space in between them letting his words trail off.

"I've been wondering if I should try and go to the Halloween party?" Devon suggested.

"If it was anyone else I would maybe try and talk you out of it. But for Em, she just gets stuck in her head. So something where you come to her would probably be helpful," Jamie said.

He seemed relieved that she was planning to reach out.

"Do you think so?"

"I think she needs to hear how serious you are about her. How much you value the relationship. But I think she's afraid."

"Afraid?"

"Yeah, I think she really likes you and that maybe she's afraid her feelings aren't reciprocated. Maybe if she talks to you it'll just lead her to heartbreak." The words were a punch to Devon's gut. She had assumed that not answering her texts were a form of anger or passive aggression not self-protection.

"We definitely need to talk. I've spent this week without her, and if nothing else I realize her place in my life."

"And what is her place in your life?" Jamie asked, arching an eyebrow.

"Oh wow, subtle brother." Devon teased.

"I wasn't going for subtle, and I still want to hear your answer," Jamie said pointedly.

"Em is so many things rolled into one for me. She's not just some girl I'm having sex with. Em is my best friend, and the only woman I want in my bed. She's my forever person." Jamie wiped a tear from his eyes.

"Are you seriously crying?" Devon asked.

"I can't help it. That was beautiful." Jamie said. Devon shook her head with a smile.

"We really need to find you a boyfriend," Devon said.

"Ewww, love." Jamie said, recoiling as if from a snake.

"You love love," Devon teased.

"For other people. Love is messy and complicated," Jamie said with a grimace.

"It's been a long time. Don't you want to find someone?" Devon asked.

"I already found someone. There's no reason to keep looking," Jamie said.

"Jamie, the breakup was years ago."

"I know, but it was real. I can't keep looking when I've already found my soulmate. But you and Em are happening right very now. This is your moment, sis. If I could go back I would find a way to make things work with Nash. I regret the way things ended, and if you don't do something big, you're going to end up with your own regrets," Jamie said resting a hand on Devon's shoulder. Devon patted his hand, her heart breaking for him a little. At least she had a chance to course correct with Em.

Jamie's words touched her. She had known that her brother was hung up on his first love, Nash Archer. This was the first time she'd been able to empathize with his feelings. The first time that she had someone in her life that she couldn't bear the thought of losing. Break-ups were always sad; they were endings after all. But Devon had always been quick to rebound. Moving on from a failed relationship had never been a problem for her, until now. Until Em. Her longest relationship had been three years, but when it ended she hadn't felt like this. Hadn't felt like there was a piece of her life missing. But Em had become so many things at one time, her lover yes, but also her best friend.

"I'm sorry if I haven't been very supportive about you and Nash. I just didn't understand until now."

"It's okay, sis. I guess the real question is what are you going to do from here?"

"I think I'm going to figure out a Halloween costume," Devon said with a grin.

"That's my girl," Jamie said with a grin. The two of them finished up lunch. Devon felt better, at least marginally. She had a plan, Devon would go to the party and lay it all on the line. If she could be completely vulnerable with Em maybe the thing between them could be real.

She ordered a costume online and hoped it would arrive by the time she got home. Classes passed by in a complete blur for the day. A swirl of people in an ever-changing background of scenery until she found herself back home. Her days had passed that way since her fight with Em. She hadn't noticed how much color and vibrance Em brought into her life until she was gone. Devon looked at her good luck jar still sitting on her mantle. The hex was gone, but without Em in her life she was far from lucky.

Chapter 21

Devon stared down at her new costume. The online ad had made the forest pixie outfit seem cuter. Her whole demeanor had shifted since buying the outfit. Was this really something she wanted to do? Was she actually going to crash Emilia's Halloween party? The definition of cliche petty, break-up behavior. Except they weren't broken up, Devon wouldn't accept that until she heard it straight from Em herself. If she went and Em told her they were done, it would be devastating. At least if Em said the words she would have an answer, instead of languishing in this awful in-between place.

As the day continued into the early evening Devon felt her nerves growing. Acid built in her stomach churning it. Her hands were shaky and Devon's heart pounded like an unsteady drum inside her chest. She needed to get dressed in her costume, instead she stared at the outfit. Devon took a deep breath, grabbed her costume and ran to put it on. The only way to make it through the night would be with tiny acts of bravery.

Once dressed Devon assessed herself in the mirror. She

looked good, the costume was a jade green that complimented both her hair and skin tone. Devon tousled her hair, letting it fall in red waves down her back. The doorbell rang announcing Jamie's arrival. She had asked, or begged him to go with her, Jamie would never allow her to chicken out. With her brother there, she was bound to be just a little bit braver.

"You all set?" Jamie asked.

"Not yet, I have to finish the aesthetic," Devon said, she pointed to her stack of makeup. Jamie rolled his eyes.

"I appreciate your team spirit," Devon yelled down the hall as she carefully applied her makeup in the bathroom.

"At this point there isn't much I wouldn't do if it means getting the two of you back on speaking terms," Jamie teased.

"Ha ha," Devon said, tone dripping with sarcasm.

When she was done, she looked every bit like a pixie. Jamie handed her his jacket, which she took. She planted her feet halting at the door.

"Jamie, what if she's not happy to see me? What if she sees me and just breaks up with me?" Jamie patted her arm.

"I've known Em for a long time. I don't think she's capable

of being that level of callous to you. But for argument's sake, if that happens… at least you leave knowing where you stand and that you did everything you could think of to make things right. Also, either way you have a cute pixie costume," Jamie said, shrugging his shoulders.

"So you're saying I win either way," Devon smiled, arching an eyebrow.

"Exactly," Jamie said. They walked out together. The crisp Fall air bit into the parts of Devon's skin that were exposed.

1111 October Lane was in full Halloween effect. There were bats and ghosts hanging from the tops of trees. Fake cobwebs lined the entryway. Quinn stood there handing out name tags at the door with markers.

"Hey guys, welcome. Just write the name of your character on the tag," Quinn said with a smile. Devon and Jamie each took a tag. On her tag Devon wrote *Pixie.* Jamie, who hadn't bothered with a costume for the night, wrote *Unironically Jamie* on his tag. Devon took one glance at his name tag and quieted a laugh.

"What?" Jamie asked.

"Just you. You're perfect." Devon said, reaching up to mess up his hair.

"That's nothing, I'm going to insist that people address me by my full tag name." Devon patted the name tag. She looked around but couldn't see Em.

"Hey, have you seen Em anywhere lately?" Devon asked Quinn.

"The last time I saw her, she was headed towards the kitchen." Quinn said.

"Go get her, tiger," Jamie said, giving Devon the slightest push forwards.

"Aren't you coming?" Devon asked.

"I can't do everything for you. Now go fly, baby bird." Jamie said, giving her a tiny hug. Devon offered him a weak smile then headed off. The kitchen had never felt so far away before, every step another obstacle to be overcome.

Devon went step by step until she was standing in front of the kitchen. Em stood in front of her, facing the opposite wall talking to a few of her guests. Devon had a lump in her throat that she thought must be her heart. To the side of her was the living room, where guests sang Karaoke over the sound system. Noise and shuffle went on around her, but all Devon saw was Em. Everything faded to black except the one person she was there to see.

Em turned and locked eyes with hers immediately. Devon froze, a deer in the headlights of an oncoming vehicle. Em stood frozen, too. For a moment they were the only ones in the kitchen. Devon saw the painful grimace sweep across Em's face. She saw Em take in a long drawn in sigh. Devon's eyes darted around and finally landed on the Karaoke machine. The simplicity of it made her smile. She shot Em her warmest smile, took in a deep breath and walked to the Karaoke Machine. Out of respect she allowed the two girls singing "Lonely Hearts" to finish, though she doubted anyone would have minded the interruption.

She grabbed the mic, allowing herself to feel the weight of the moment. Em was still in the kitchen, leaned against the wall that led to the living room and watching. She was watching Devon, and for a moment she lost her ability to speak. Her heart caught in her throat; Devon forced herself to focus. She gave lectures all day long but faced with the woman she loved, the mic shook in her hand.

"I'm sorry to interrupt the party. I promise this will only take a minute. Not long ago I said something that hurt someone who is very important to me. Em, I wanted to take a minute to explain exactly what you mean to me. We only recently became friends, but you are my best friend. When I have good news, you're the first person I want to text about it. When something bad happens you're the first person I want to call, the first voice I want to hear. You wanted to know what I want us to be. My answer is that you're my forever person. The only person I want to wake up next to every day for all my days." Devon couldn't see Em, she was lost in the shifting crowd around her. Or perhaps she had listened and left. Devon handed the mic back to the nearest person in line and stepped away. As she turned, she nearly ran straight into Em.

Em didn't say anything. She didn't need words, the tears in her eyes were enough. Devon opened her mouth, but Em threw her arms around her. Em effectively killed whatever Devon had been about to say. Instead, Devon sank deep into Em's embrace. The feel of Em's arms around her, the scent of her shampoo as they each continued to pull one another deeper.

Devon didn't have exact words to describe the feel of it. All she knew was that she didn't want the moment to end. Everything she had been hoping for was right in front of her. All the pain of the past few days unwound inside of her. She felt hot wet tears slide down her face. Em pulled away first and Devon had to fight the urge to pull her back. They looked at each other for a long moment before Em reached up, wiping Devon's tears away with a finger. She took Devon's hand and led her through the crowd. It took Devon a minute to realize that Em was leading her upstairs to her room. Devon felt the tightness in her chest loosen, Em's room was a place of safety and quiet. She hadn't realized until that moment how much she had missed this place, how much she had missed Em.

Chapter 22

Em couldn't believe Devon was here. With her. In her room. A swirl of thoughts entered her mind. She found herself leaning against her doorframe for support. In the days since their fight Em had assumed that her relationship with Devon was through. *Insignificant,* that word didn't mean serious or profound. Em had needed to face the facts that she wasn't looking for something insignificant. Em wanted serious, and she deserved it. She had thought that Devon must not want those things. Yet here she was. Devon Willis had come to her house and told everyone within earshot how much she cared.

The gesture was more than Em had expected. Em had spent the past several days conflicted, positive that things between her and Devon were over. Convincing herself that they wanted different things. But Devon had shown up and done all the legwork to show her how much the thing between them meant to her.

"So," Devon said in an attempt to break the silence.

"So," Em said as she crossed the space between them. Her arms wound around Devon's neck pulling her in. She kissed Devon hard on the mouth, trying to pour every ounce of want she'd felt since their fight into that one gesture. Devon entered into the kiss tentatively, before giving in completely. Em felt Devon surging forward, giving all of herself. Their lips stayed locked together even as their tongues wrestled inside their mouths.

Em's hands slipped down Devon's costume, trying desperately to find where it ended. She wanted nothing more than to remove the fabric that was between them. Her fingers longed to touch Devon's bare skin. Nimble fingers meant that she reached her destination quickly, pulling the costume carefully over Devon's head. Goosebumps shivered up Devon's body at Em's touch. Em watched them appear and smiled.

She reached behind Devon and undid her bra, watching as it fell casually to the floor. There was a loud knock at the door, followed by it being flung wide open. Surprised, Devon leapt forward, Em shielded her in an embrace. Jamie's voice rang loudly through the room as he stepped across the threshold.

"Guys, everyone is talking about you downstairs. They say that the two of you are...." Jamie's words trailed off as he registered what sort of moment he had walked in on.

"Jamie, what the hell?" Devon half shouted. The sight of his sister in partial undress made a bright red blush spread through Jamie's cheeks.

"I, I... Oh, jeez. I was just excited," Jamie stammered. Em pinched the bridge of her nose.

"We know you had great intentions. Why don't you wait for us downstairs at the party," Em suggested, her tone was not harsh but firm. The words seemed to bring Jamie back to the present moment.

"Right. Absolutely," Jamie said. He ran, not walked, from the room. Em closed the door behind him. Devon put her face in her hands.

"Well, that just happened." Devon said.

"It did. Sorry. I didn't realize I needed to lock my bedroom door."

"When Jamie is around no safety measure is too great."

"It seems I have underestimated your brother."

"That's more common than you think. He's constantly breaking expectations. He's been super bummed since we had our fight." Em tensed, and she saw Devon register the motion. She had known they would make their way to talking about the fight. Em had just hoped for a few more good moments before they got there. But Jamie had broken that spell, and the time had arrived sooner than she had hoped.

"There's been a lot of the bummed feeling going around since then," Em said.

"Can I ask you a question?" Devon asked, her tone more timid than Em liked to hear. She raised her green eyes to meet Devon's gaze.

"Of course, you can ask me anything," Em said, her nervousness more evident than she liked.

"Why didn't you answer any of my text messages?" Devon asked, this time her voice had a pained edginess to it that Em liked even less. She hated to think that she had caused Devon any pain.

"I was afraid," Em said, with a simple shrug of the shoulders looking down at her shoes.

"Afraid?" Devon asked.

"I was afraid that once I responded we'd be done for good. I thought just letting everything slip away would be better. That it would hurt less than hearing you say you weren't ready for a commitment. Or that being with me had been fun, but that maybe this thing between us had run its course. I've heard all those lines before, and they hurt. But I thought if I heard you say something like that to me, my heart might not recover from it. I knew we'd have to talk eventually, but I thought maybe we could delay it," Em said. She felt hot tears form behind her eyes, but she refused to let them fall.

"Didn't you think that maybe we wanted the exact same things? Didn't you think maybe I wanted a chance at forever with you? That maybe I have the same fears?"

"No, I didn't. Because you're Devon Willis and I'm just Emilia Thorne..." Em began, but Devon cut her off short.

"High school was a long time ago. I'm not who I used to be, and neither are you. We're different and better. We've had time to grow into ourselves. And who I am very much likes you. Who I am spent the last several days scared and sad because I thought I had lost my chance at forever love. I thought I had lost my person," Devon said, voice going up an octave. Em watched as tears spilled from Devon's eyes. Seeing the tears fall was more than Em could bear, her own tears fell from her eyes. She wrapped her arms around Devon, bringing her in close once again. Em slid a strand of Devon's hair behind her ear and whispered,

"I'm so sorry. I'm sorry that I didn't believe in you and what we have together. I'm so sorry that I didn't let you explain. I wanted to talk to you, I truly did. But every time I thought about reaching out I just heard you saying that we weren't significant. Then my fear would get the better of me. I promise that from now on I will give you the benefit of the doubt." Em's words touched Devon's heart. She felt Devon bury her face in her neck, ending the gesture with a kiss.

"I love you," Devon whispered.

"And I love you," Em returned. Her heart exploded in her chest. Devon didn't just like her, she loved her. And she didn't want to just spend time with Em, Devon wanted forever. Em wanted those things too, she longed for a forever with Devon. She closed her eyes and let her mind wander, letting her intuition picture what their lives could be.

In that moment Em saw flashes of Christmases under a big tree in the living room, with a fire in the fireplace. She saw nights spent watching the stars from the deck, Devon's socked feet resting in her lap. There were birthdays, and Halloweens, and someday children. At the end their two wrinkled hands stayed clasped together as they sat on the porch watching the night sky together.

The images built onto one another. A love story waiting to be written. A love story waiting to be lived. And they got to live it together. This moment was the beginning of something much more profound and beautiful than anything she could have imagined. Em opened her eyes, hugging Devon closer than ever before. She had seen it, their life together. Had seen their forever story, and it was beautiful.

Chapter 23

EPILOGUE

Devon paced around the house. Six months ago she had moved into Em's house, now their home.

Within the first three months Devon had known. She didn't get flashes, or intuition the way Em did, but she had been certain of her life with Em all the same.

Last month she had bought a ring and given it to Jamie for safekeeping. It was bad enough dating someone who inexplicably knew things, without adding the possibility of Em stumbling across the ring. She had been waiting for just the right moment and today was the day. Spring was in full effect. Everything was new, blooming or waiting to be born. The perfect time to start a new chapter with Em. The front door swung open without warning. Devon jumped out of her skin as Jamie entered.

"Seriously, Jamie, what the fuck?" Devon shouted, her hand clutching her chest in surprise.

"What? Em gave me a key years ago," Jamie offered with a casual shrug.

"I mean great, but knock first before you just barge in here. You almost gave me a heart attack."

"Okay, you're right. I'm just so excited."

"I know. Me too. Did you bring the ring?"

"Of course, it's here in the box." Jamie said, pulling a ring box from his pants. Devon flipped it open, double-checking on the ring. She breathed a subtle sigh of relief when it was inside.

"So, what are you planning?" Jamie asked.

"I can't tell you yet." Devon laughed.

"What do you mean?" Jamie said crestfallen.

"I won't know until it's time."

"Ugh." Jamie groaned.

"Okay, that's enough of that. You gotta get out of here before she comes home."

"Wait. But…"

"I promise you'll be the first one who gets details," Devon

said. Jamie slumped his shoulders, looking down at his shoes.

"Oh, come on, you know you're important to us both," Devon said, giving him a large squeeze. Jamie lit a smile across his face.

"I know. I know. Okay, have a great time tonight. Make it spectacular," Jamie teased.

"Great, nice to know there isn't any pressure."

"No pressure. I just want it to be perfect for you and her," Jamie said with a teasing grin.

"Jamie!" Devon gave a whine.

"I'm kidding. It's going to be great. I mean how could it not be?"

"Thank you. Now get out of here before you stick your foot in your mouth again," Devon said, giving her brother a hug on his way out the door.

Alone in the house Devon sat on the couch, feeling the weight of the night ahead of her. She had a whole scene planned. Devon had bought orange and purple string lights. It made her think of Halloween time, all those months ago when she and Em had started dating. Em had confided in her that she wished that she could keep string lights up year round. Tonight, Devon wanted to make that a reality. She brought down Em's telescope and set it up on the deck. Em would be home late; she and Violet were doing inventory at Natural Wonders. Devon set everything up, showered, cooked, and waited.

Her heart skipped a few beats when the lights from Em's car showed through the window. She heard the car door close and Em's key turn in the lock. Devon fought against the urge to run to her. Em closed the door and surveyed the scene in front of her. The string lights gave the house a hazy glow. On the table sat a freshly cooked meal. Devon thought she may have seen Em gasp.

"What's all this?" Em asked, meeting her eyes. Devon felt a heat spread through her body, an unquenchable fire that was all too common around Em.

"I know you worked hard all day, and I wanted to do something special."

"I would say you've outdone yourself." Em said, with a smile. She walked over to Devon pulling her in close.

"Not even close. Not where you're concerned." Devon kissed Em along the neck. She forced herself to stop, not allowing herself to go too far.

They ate the grilled chicken with rice that Devon had prepared. Em sat at the table, her warmest smile across her face.

"What's next?" Em asked.

"Come with me." Devon took Em by the hand leading her to the deck. Em's eyes landed on the telescope, her smile widened immediately.

"You brought down the telescope."

"Well, you always talk about how much you wish you remembered to bring it downstairs more. Besides, tonight's sky is supposed to be very clear." Em adjusted the telescope then looked through it. While she busied herself Devon took out the ring and dropped to one knee beside her.

"It's beautiful, you have to see this," Em said. When she turned her head and saw Devon, she covered her mouth with a hand. In the ring box a heart-cut Sunstone caught the moonlight at just the right angle to show off its color.

"Is that a Sunstone?"

"I knew they were your favorite; I didn't think a diamond would do the trick." Em chuckled even as hot tears flowed down her cheeks.

"Em, I know I'm not psychic. But my vision of our lives together is clearer than anything I've ever experienced. I can't imagine my life any other way except with you in it. I want all my memories going forward to include you. Will you please marry me?" Em's tears flowed freely.

"I can't believe you did all of this. Of course, I'll marry you." Em pulled Devon to her feet. Devon expected an embrace but was surprised when she saw Em digging in her own pocket. Em pulled out a box and sank to her own knee. She opened her box to reveal an Aquamarine stone in the middle of a rose gold band.

"You're not going to believe this, but I've been trying for days to propose. I can't believe you beat me to it. Devon, ever since you came back into my life you've brought the magic back. I can't wait to live out our love story one day at a time. Will you marry me?" Devon choked on her own tears.

"Yes, every day, yes." Devon said, throwing her arms around Em.

"Have you really been trying to propose for days?" Devon asked.

"I was trying to find the right moment. But you made the

right moment happen and that's what I love about you." Em pulled Devon in for another kiss.

"I think the way this happened was perfect. We both chose each other. I can't imagine a better moment." Devon said between kisses. Em pulled away suddenly.

"Wait a minute did Jamie know about you and the ring?" Em asked.

"Actually yeah, he's been keeping the ring for me so that you wouldn't find it. Did he know about yours?"

"He knew." Em chuckled, playfully throwing her hands in the air.

"Jamie is better at keeping secrets than I thought," Devon said with a laugh.

"Right! What other secrets is he hiding?" Em asked pointedly.

"Definitely best not to ask." Devon grabbed Em around the waist pulling her body in as close as possible. She brought her head closer to Em, until their foreheads rested against one another.

Em's dark hair fell around them, a curtain protecting

them from the outside world. A perfect point in time. Em's hand found Devon's cheek guiding her in for a kiss. Long and deep, the kiss filling them both with passion for the night to come. Their bodies knew this dance and fit together perfectly. Devon's hands slid around cupping Em's ass, still pulling Em in.

Em took Devon's finger and slid the Aquamarine ring onto her finger. Devon followed suit sliding the Sunstone ring over Em's knuckle. They grabbed one another's hands as they allowed their kiss to continue. It would progress to other things Devon knew. Right now, nothing could be more perfect than kissing Em under the night sky, the stars providing them with the best backdrop they could ask for. Their hands were as intertwined as their lips. Devon marveled, still unsure how her life had wound up here. How had she ended up in this place with this person? All she could feel was grateful, and lucky. They had created the most beautiful love. A love story that they would continue to write every day for the rest of their lives.

More by Jenn Bridges:

Nashville Love Series:

Nashville in Love

Music City Romance

Forever in Nashville

Longing in Nashville

WaterColor Romance Series:

Love Along the Way

Borrowed Hearts

Finding Forever Series:

Chasing Forever

Printed in Great Britain
by Amazon

10279130R00129